RECEIVED

JUL 26 2021

BROADVIEW LIBRARY

NO LONGER PROPERTY OF
SEATTLE PUBLIC LIBRARY

'Employing a language that is sharp, concise and visceral, [Consiglio shows] his talent as a natural storyteller, a social chronicler, and as a poet of some refinement.'
Morning Star

'His stories are told with dispassionate realism while being varnished with a surrealist gloss, creating his own in-between style (...). Poetic turns reminiscent of Pablo Neruda erupt within the narrative.'
Culture Trip

'[Consiglio] carves out a singular space by focusing on characters who do not quite have a place of their own.'
Full Stop

'Everyone should write with fury. Everyone should write like Jorge Consiglio.' **Ricardo Piglia**

'Consiglio is a robust writer, a writer who deeply interests me.'
Beatriz Sarlo

'*Fate* is a book of beautiful human intensity.'
Flavia Pitella.

'There is something indescribable in the meticulousness of the patience and beauty that Consiglio brings into play in his writing. Something impossible to put into words and which, therefore, can only be revealed in the fervour of enthusiasm.'
Eugenia Almeida

'*Fate* deals with all those things that don't last, the contrast between the permanence of objects and the things that vanish: a glance from a train, casual sex in a hotel, that word you wanted to say but couldn't, a musical note; everything that won't remain in a battle against that which will survive us: the city, the streets, the empty glass of beer.'
Gabriela Borrelli

'*Fate* narrates what it's like to meet someone and to build something from that encounter; what it's like to leave somebody, to be left by someone and confirm the end of love. (...) Offering a crushing premise – "There are things that start by chance but never come to an end" – *Fate* narrates the way in which things happen and how each of us experiences that.'
Martín Kohan

FATE

CHARCO PRESS

First published by Charco Press 2020

Charco Press Ltd., Office 59, 44-46 Morningside Road, Edinburgh
EH10 4BF

Copyright © Jorge Consiglio 2018

First published in Spanish as *Tres monedas* by Eterna Cadencia (Argentina)
English translation copyright © Carolina Orloff & Fionn Petch 2020

The rights of Jorge Consiglio to be identified as the author of this work and
of Carolina Orloff and Fionn Petch to be identified as the translators of this
work have been asserted by them in accordance with the Copyright, Designs
and Patents Act 1988.

Work published with funding from the 'Sur' Translation Support Programme
of the Ministry of Foreign Affairs of Argentina / Obra editada en el marco
del Programa 'Sur' de Apoyo a las Traducciones del Ministerio de Relaciones
Exteriores y Culto de la República Argentina.

All rights reserved. This book is copyright material and must not be copied,
reproduced, transferred, distributed, leased, licensed or publicly performed or
used in any way except as specifically permitted in writing by the publisher, as
allowed under the terms and conditions under which it was purchased or as
strictly permitted by the applicable copyright law. Any unauthorised distri-
bution or use of this text may be a direct infringement of the author's and
publisher's rights, and those responsible may be liable in law accordingly.

A CIP catalogue record for this book is available from the British Library.

ISBN: 9781999368463
e-book: 9781916277823

www.charcopress.com

Edited by Robin Myers
Cover design by Pablo Font
Typeset by Laura Jones
Proofread by Fiona Mackintosh

2 4 6 8 10 9 7 5 3 1

Supported using public funding by
ARTS COUNCIL
ENGLAND

LOTTERY FUNDED

Jorge Consiglio

FATE

Translated by
Carolina Orloff & Fionn Petch

CHARCO PRESS

AUTHOR'S NOTE

The key question is: fate or chance? Life presents itself as a series of events, and we will never know if we are fulfilling a pre-established path or if fortuitousness – the accidental in the strictest sense of the word – is the decisive factor. When tragedy strikes, there is always someone who is spared by some tiny detail. As a result, triviality takes on monumental dimensions. A few years ago, there was an accident in the main railway station in Buenos Aires: the brakes failed on a suburban train and fifty-one people died. I heard the account of a woman who missed the train because she slept in. And of someone else who hadn't caught it because he lost a contact lens on his way to work. Their lives were saved. It's that simple: they saved their lives. Fate or chance? Science addresses the question through variables and proportions: what is the probability that a given event will actually occur? As we know, quantifying the world brings peace to the soul. But mathematical arguments never satisfy anyone.

Beyond all the precautions taken, beyond everything we do to protect ourselves in society, beyond personal defence mechanisms, every human being stands face-to-face with the unknown. This is the distinctive and most genuine characteristic of our species. This idea lies at the core of *Fate*. There are four characters: a taxidermist, a meteorologist, a musician and a child.

Their paths cross. They move through a city that seems to force them to take decisions: speed, in this day and age, is a value. The characters deploy infinite tenderness, yet at the same time appear implacable, as if on the very brink of themselves. They are in constant motion. They catch glimpses of beauty and love, and these inklings justify them somehow, spurring them to act. All four unknowingly make their way into the eye of a hurricane. Each of them, with both desperation and enchantment, advances towards a personal understanding of the future.

The plot of *Fate* is simple, the prose straightforward. Yet beneath this simplicity, a turbulent ocean swells. In this novel, each action is what it is – and is also something else. Or more precisely, each action is many things at once. Each sentence (the English translation is impeccable and captures every nuance of the original) reverberates, seeks to expand and transform itself into both a proposition and an enigma. When I wrote the book, one of the things I was mulling over was how to capture the intimacy of poetry. I mean the imagery: the meshing of meanings evoked by the opacity of language. That was my idea. I had other intentions, too: I imagined, for example, that the characters would find themselves in a state of solitude, would be defined by it – yet would also fight tirelessly to make that modest leap of exceptionality and intensity.

I wrote *Fate* over the course of a single scorching summer. Not a soul was left in Buenos Aires. I spent the evenings, the air conditioning on full blast, watching 1950s noir films, and discovered *The Third Man* by Carol Reed. I became fascinated by it and watched it three times over. In one scene, the two main characters, played by Orson Welles and Joseph Cotten, are talking inside a Ferris wheel cabin as it climbs into the sky. They say terrible things to each other. Welles is pitiless. I found a certain essence in this dialogue, a particular quality I sought to reproduce in the text. I don't mean the specific content of the conversation, but rather an atmosphere. I started writing with this detail in mind: in the sequence I discovered the sound that would allow the story to take form. In other words, the scene helped me finish devising the plot. This element may not even be visible on the surface, but it remains the most significant aspect of the text. The image of Cotten and Welles, arguing at the top of the wheel, gave me the tone that I imagined as the ideal acoustics of my story.

Without question, writing is a blind endeavour. Yet sometimes, when luck is on our side, we chance on signs that are enormously useful in orienting us amid this nebulous universe of possibilities.

Jorge Consiglio
Buenos Aires, November 2019

*'…understand that this world is not ruled
by immutable laws; that it is vulnerable,
uncertain. Understand that fate replaces destiny.'*

Ezequiel Martínez Estrada

Amer mixed onion, tomato and avocado. He added salt, pepper, oil and lemon. Nothing special. Just a quick snack. A guacamole. He spread it over a piece of toast and ate it slowly. He had reverted to his habit of standing while eating. He took his time to chew. He savoured the acidity while he let his mind catch in a tangle of ideas that, after a few minutes, wove together, generating a kind of atmosphere, something vague yet as vividly present as the taste of onion now dancing in his mouth.

A light bulb hung above his head. The boiler to the right, the fridge to the left. He hadn't eaten a thing in six hours. He took a sip of red wine. He hesitated, then added a couple of squirts from the soda siphon. He took a quick inhalation of air through his nose – a sigh in reverse – and in this action, as with everything he did that night, pleasure prevailed. Each occurrence, however small and insignificant, was lit by the gleam of celebration. Everything fastened together in a joyful line. Something unstoppable: a chain of wise choices and well-being.

He had spent the afternoon working on a brocket deer. It was a small animal and it was in very good shape. Its fur remained unruffled, its snout still pink; only the corneas attested to the final violence. Amer had fulfilled his tasks in strict silence since the age of ten. He blinked rarely, almost never: his tear film was remarkably resilient. What's more, his everyday work, the toil that paid the bills, justified it; that is, it gave him a reason to live. Amer was delicate: his fingertips were chrysalid-like, as if made of gauze. He was also extremely neat. Neat and delicate, two qualities hugely appreciated in his profession. He believed in giving the benefit of the doubt, in taking things slow, in the steadiness of habit.

As per usual, after work, he stood in front of his TV, remote control in hand. The brightness of the screen, its pyrotechnics, was simply spectacular. He flicked from channel to channel. He did this for a while, attentive to the light alone. The images lasted only a few seconds: a male broadcaster in shorts, a set of retractable claws, a crowd, the snowy peak of Cocuy, a plate of food, three aeroplanes up in the air, a plant growing, a building in Richmond, Saturn, the seas of the Moon, Saturn, fish gills, a weather graphic in all its splendour. Yet only one thing persisted in his mind: the image of a brown bear, hibernating. It was a huge beast, but its body still suggested the clumsy movements of a cub. It looked gentle. One of its eyes, the left, was barely open and through it, through that slit, bright as a spark, flashed menace, pure irrationality. Lingering on the image of the bear, Amer went into the kitchen, sharpened a knife against a second blade, and began chopping onions.

She wasn't sure they were ants. They were certainly tiny insects, moving aimlessly, yet very fast. Marina Kezelman grimaced in disgust. Kneeling down, wearing a pair of running shoes and rolled-up trousers, a torch clenched between her teeth, she looked like a mad explorer. She shone the light into the crevice between the wall and the fridge. It was a narrow, mournful space: the scene of a hidden world.

Marina Kezelman stretched her right arm as far as she could – the cartilage made a noise as it tensed – and moved it around in the dark. Then she overcame her revulsion, clenched her fist and struck hard. She killed ten or twenty of the insects. The survivors rustled frantically. Marina Kezelman was clearly a threat. Her height became apparent when she stood up, which she did in two movements. She was five feet four inches tall. This fact was relevant to a feature of her personality, perhaps the most significant one: her determination. Marina Kezelman was someone who faced her problems head-on. As her husband put it, she crushed them. Right now, although she was pressed for time, she decided to take action. She left the torch on the counter and opened the cupboard. She searched and searched some more. She pushed aside a pack of candles; a can of WD-40 fell from her hands. She didn't find what she was looking for, but she kept searching anyway. In the end, she got creative and sprayed the bugs with fabric stiffener. Bewilderment engulfed the community, and yet all its members continued to throng, covered in bright white foam. Marina Kezelman didn't know what to do next. She bit down hard on her lower lip, knelt for the third time and stormed them blindly. She flattened over a hundred with her bare hand. Death writ large – this longed-for massacre – filled her with elation, a state of excitement. She rubbed her forehead and continued her mission, but the impulse faded after ten seconds. With an over-hasty swipe of her hand, she snagged one of her fingernails in a crack in the wall and it broke. A rush of cold rippled up her spine. She let out a short shriek of pain and ran to the bathroom. For three seconds (no longer than three seconds) she became aware that a neighbour – an eighteen-year-old kid she'd seen around – had started to play the first chords of a Dvorak polka on the piano. The battle against the bugs had reached a ceasefire.

Everything was equally important in his head. He struggled to get organised. On the second Wednesday of July, he found himself walking down Cerrito Street with a fellow musician from the orchestra. They had just spent three hours at the Colón Opera House rehearsing a piece by Weber. Now they were relaxed, still flush with a sense of accomplishment. They were enjoying the sun and their shared indifference to the anxious traffic. Broadly speaking, their stories were similar: both of them came from small towns; both were third-generation musicians; both had started families in Buenos Aires. Karl was German; the other, Santiago, was Colombian. They were delighted with the city's culinary offerings. They mentioned an Italian place that was said to have the best lasagne in town, as well as a steak house in the Monserrat neighbourhood. They spoke as if they were experts in beef cuts, cooking temperatures and pairing meat with different types of wine. They were making an effort. They were showing off what they knew, and their fervent language somehow bolstered their words. They were used to tracking their own rhythms. They were enraptured by their topics of discussion, but also by the register – the tone, the cadence – of their own voices. They were actual voice boxes. This is how they worked.

They had their musical instruments with them: Karl's oboe, Santiago's viola. They crossed Lavalle Street. And a few metres from the corner, they ran into a group of schoolgirls in their tartan skirts. The girls were blocking their way as they milled outside a newsagent. The pavement was wide, but the two musicians decided to step down onto the road to circumvent them. Karl adjusted the strap of his oboe case. And in that very instant, he realised that one of the girls – he was struck by her beauty as she distractedly handed a hundred-peso note to a schoolmate – reminded him of his eldest daughter, whom he hadn't seen in five years. Five years, he said out loud, but the noisy exhaust of a passing bus drowned him out. The city adapted to even the most intimate moments. Karl had a vision: the girl's hair – a compact mass – had a life of its own, independent from the rest of her body.

He'd planned to say goodbye at the corner of Corrientes Avenue, but something indefinite – the balmy weather, the pleasant conversation – made him change his mind. They decided to step into a bar. A long counter, five tables in a row. They ordered black coffee and regular sandwiches, which were brought to them toasted, but didn't complain. It even amused them, the mistake. The sound of a radio began to filter through the background noise. The light streaming in from the street got tangled in Karl's hair before it spilled onto the table. Mostly they spoke about Germany. Karl detailed his routine as a conservatory student in Dresden. His account was administrative in tone: the day as a succession of demands. Suddenly, the electric drone of the radio seemed to sharpen and take on shape. It was a bolero. Karl abruptly changed the subject. Somehow, he found his phone in his hand. He brought up pictures of his wife, Marina Kezelman. She's a meteorologist, he said. She's got a postgraduate degree from the National Research Institute, he added. She's had a government job for seven months now. Sometimes, she travels to different provinces to assess the weather conditions in desert areas. She's part of an interdisciplinary team. The Colombian finished his sandwich in a single gulp. Seen from outside, the musicians sketched an old-fashioned scene. There was something unsettling about them. They were characters from another era.

A mistake. Her mind was elsewhere as she walked down Sarmiento Street. All of a sudden, there she was, tripping over the wares a street vendor was flogging from a square of tarp. The guy had been waiting his entire life for this opportunity. He screamed blue murder. Marina Kezelman prepared her defence – bulldog face and counter-attack – but when she saw that things were turning nasty and noted the indifference of the passers-by, she lowered her gaze, shrinking back as if she were at fault. She walked on for another two blocks under the sun, the collar of her shirt turned slightly upwards.

She stopped at a lottery booth on Corrientes. She looked at the tickets on display and burst into tears. A bespectacled hipster guy asked her if she was ok. Marina couldn't catch her breath to reply. She washed her face in the toilets of La Ópera café and rushed to her chiropractic session. She'd had a pain in her neck for two months now and a friend had suggested this practice. She was seen by a very tall woman who had hair just like an aunt of hers who'd died a decade earlier. Marina Kezelman didn't believe in coincidences, and so she was stunned when the therapist said her first name was Julia: her dead aunt's name. She didn't say a word. She lay down on the bed, closed her eyes and let the woman work on her back. She left with a sensation of relief and mild lumbar pain. Julia had warned her that some temporary side effects were to be expected. Marina Kezelman clung to those words. She stopped thinking about her body and carried on towards Rivadavia Avenue.

Twenty minutes later, she was in a café. A macchiato with toast and jam. She'd taken a table next to a mirror. Marina's movements were deft, assured. It was her style, a bearing that, deep down, she considered aristocratic: she refused to associate time with productivity. Serene, she ate. Every now and then, she turned her head to the left, unable to resist her own reflection. She fixed her hair – a lock at her temple – and checked her face for marks of time. Her chin had receded, her cheeks had gained in volume. Her eyes were still the same almond shape, but they had gradually sunk into their orbits. Marina Kezelman was an attractive woman and this fact, evident to the world and no secret to her, had planted in her psyche – as far back as her early teenage years – a confidence that had allowed her to get whatever she wanted. She would choose a direction and move forward, with a certain degree of bewilderment, but always forward.

Taking her last sip of coffee, she noticed that a guy at the counter was looking at her. He was young and wearing a pair of beige trousers. At first it bothered her, his stare, but she soon joined in the game. Kezelman understood that she was the main character in a story. The light shone on her directly, brought out her nose, made her look pale. As soon as she realised this, she shifted. She sat with her back as straight as possible and touched a finger softly to her lips. She pretended to be distracted by the movement of the afternoon, the passing cars and people. Once in position, she checked the man's reaction. He was talking with the bartender but still paying attention to her. Standing at the counter, he was like a fish in water. He fulfilled his allotted role without objection. Marina Kezelman reminded herself that you should never give everything away. She swallowed a morsel and mentally reviewed all her son's activities. She toyed with the idea of infidelity. This guy was uncharted territory. She checked her phone. Not long ago she'd downloaded an I Ching app that she consulted from time to time. She wanted to face the future in the best possible conditions. She took her time to formulate the question, but the reply threw her. She wasn't familiar with the set of symbolic codes, the visuals, the ideas. She ordered another coffee, black this time, and re-read the text three times. She was still stuck with a couple of images she struggled to interpret as the moment of truth approached.

What shall I do? she wondered. She went for the stable option. She paid with her Visa card and left a banknote as a tip. She tore outside like a whirlwind. The chances of the guy following her were negligible, but just in case, she donned her grimmest expression. She hurried for two blocks, her heels clicking, and went into a hardware store. She asked for ant poison. Give me the strongest one you've got, she said. She was shown a gel bait and an ivory-coloured powder. The shop assistant claimed that this combination was foolproof. Persuaded, she purchased both. She felt certain that, over the afternoon, things – as if of their own volition – had lined up in her favour.

At fourteen, Amer had raised a cigarette to his lips and swallowed the smoke. He'd been told not to, but at that age he was stubborn and wanted to try everything. His chin sported a few sparse hairs. Every so often he would stroke them, checking on them, keeping them alive. It was the first evidence of puberty. Literally, on that day, he had swallowed smoke. Then, he'd stepped away to cough. Truth be told, he was the one who'd been swallowed up. For a moment, he thought he was going to die. Simple as that. And he had accepted it with a certain peace. It was two in the afternoon. Spring. Mild weather. He was in a plaza, under the shadow cast by the bust of Eloy Alfaro. From that day until he turned fifty-four – with a few interruptions – Amer had smoked. Way too much. Now his legs would get heavy, he'd get short of breath. He had to quit; there was no getting round it. A doctor made the decision for him. A couple of his arteries were blocked, the doctor determined. Percutaneous coronary intervention. As he talked, Amer was distracted by the dust particles suspended in a ray of sunshine. He tried to think back: it'd been a year since he'd left the city limits.

The campaign began. He searched online for places that dealt with addictions, but none of them persuaded him. The answer came from somewhere unexpected: a forum for taxidermists that took place once a fortnight. A guy from Córdoba who lived in Buenos Aires told him he had the same problem. Sharing a self-help group would be a good solution.

One Tuesday, they went together to the Tobar García psychiatric hospital for children. They were met by a doctor with a Basque surname – Eizaga – who wordlessly obliged them to sit in a semi-circle with other people. The smell of floor cleaning products was overpowering. At first, Amer felt awkward. He wriggled in his chair, his legs itched. To his right, a 150-kilo guy breathed heavily. He gave off a sweet odour, like that of a nectarine compote, which mixed with the aroma of disinfectant. Eizaga said that an adult inhales and exhales between five and six litres of air per minute. This fact was essential to what he went on to explain, yet Amer lost the thread immediately. He didn't catch a single word. He was elsewhere. A woman across from him was biting her nails. Her image, even when still, was dynamic. She shifted from one geometrical plane to another with utter spontaneity, as if her desire depended on this exhaltation. Amer couldn't grasp what he was seeing. And so, as always, he veered towards simplification. I am interested in that woman, he said to himself, which put an end to the issue. He simply erased it and moved on to something else. At the end of the session, he learned that the woman's name was Clara and that she was ten years younger than him.

The guy from Córdoba gave Amer a ride home. They drove down Ramón Carrillo Avenue and talked, among other things, about what they had just experienced. Each elaborated on his point of view, which didn't fully coincide with the other's. But they both agreed that good judgement was no match for the hegemony of pleasure.

The Colombian disappeared into the subway. Karl walked down Corrientes towards Pueyrredón. He was taller than everyone else. He crossed Uruguay Street and stopped short in front of a bookshop. His eye roved over the window display before he carried on. Marina Kezelman was turning forty in two weeks and he wanted a gift that would surprise her. They had met in a bar in Madrid a decade before. Everything had happened very quickly. Moved by desire and, above all, an exaggerated sense of honesty, they'd made their decisions.

Packing up his personal mythology, two suitcases and an oboe, Karl moved to Argentina. Those were tough times, although their intimate harmony gave them the best outlook on the world, the most benevolent one. Their relationship in those days – its complexity, its refuge – made them indestructible. They sensed this and made the most of it: they found work, moved to a central neighbourhood and had a son, Simón. Now Karl wanted to give Marina Kezelman something that would be worthy of their mutual understanding. But nothing occurred to him. He meandered round town for longer than he had planned and, almost without realising, he arrived at Callao Avenue. It was a strange day for Karl. More than ever before, he felt the city had changed him; at the same time, he noticed that the change hadn't affected the core of his personality. In other words, Karl was someone else but also himself. This fact – so obscure that he found it hard to put into words – materialised in a blurry and seemingly unfounded sorrow which was hard to shake off. He stopped by a newspaper stand to wait for the green light, and when it came, he carried on walking. Halfway across the avenue, an image of barbecued short ribs flashed into his mind, neither overcooked nor rare. This image made him instantly and voraciously hungry. Karl knew himself well: his appetite was boundless. To some extent he liked this trait of his; he saw it as a positive part of himself – joyful, celebratory even, to describe it somehow. For a second, he thought about making a stop at a pizza place, but settled for something much simpler. He bought two chocolate bars at a corner store and wolfed them down. From that point on, his pace slowed ever so slightly. Food, as per usual, started him on a meditative path. This time, it proved fruitful: he hit on the perfect gift for his wife. I've got it, he said to himself. He checked his phone and confirmed he was at the right place. He walked two blocks down Corrientes and entered a sex shop. He browsed for a while. Despite knowing exactly what he wanted, he felt confused. The solution came when a sales assistant volunteered the necessary information. He left the shop with an orange vibrator offering twelve and a half centimetres of penetration.

Once back on the street, the atmosphere had changed. Everything was charged with a certain immediacy. Karl walked quickly, as if he were late, and with two strides leapt onto a bus. He knew there was no one at home (Marina Kezelman had taken their son to swimming lessons). Even so, he entered cautiously. He chewed on three coffee beans and started to pace, his thoughts whirring, partly distracted and partly worried. He decided to hide the vibrator in his son's room. He unwrapped it and placed it in a plastic box they used to store cast-off toys. He made a cup of tea, squeezing half a lemon into the cup, and Skyped a friend in Germany. He learned that in Olching, a town of 25,000 people west of Munich, it had been raining for a whole week.

She pushed. She pushed with all her might and succeeded in moving the fridge twenty centimetres. Marina Kezelman was gifted with an extraordinary physical strength. She'd been into athletics as a teenager. Athletics had toned her legs – her abductor muscles were perfectly defined – and taught her to ration her energy. Her stamina was exceptional. She never lacked vigour. That very day, a cloudy Saturday, she'd been up since 7 a.m. She'd prepared breakfast for Simón and immersed herself in an Excel graph, plotting humidity metrics of a forest in the northern province of Chaco, near the Pilcomayo river. On the graph, the curve – a green line connecting twelve points – was ascending. Kezelman verified that all the data was correct. Sorted! she exclaimed out loud.

She was researching the link between humidity and the growth of a particular herb – a variety of wild chamomile – that exhibited a direct relationship with the reproduction rate of rabbits in the area. The survey was done using satellite imagery, but on occasion she went out into the field. Closing her laptop, she checked on her son and went to put some coffee on. From the kitchen window, she could see people standing at the bus stop. She brought her fingers to her lips as if she were holding a cigarette and shifted her gaze. By chance, she noticed two ants on a tile, to the left of the cupboard. She swept them away with a single stroke of her hand. At once she went to examine the side of the fridge. The nest was swarming. Marina Kezelman instantly asked herself a thousand questions, yet all of them, in one way or another, were focused on resolving the same enigma: what were those damn bugs feeding on in a kitchen like hers?

She acted as she'd been advised. She moved the fridge to improve the angle of attack, sprinkled the poison and placed the bait at strategic points. As she washed her hands, she decided to order an Uber to the airport in the morning. A trip to the northern province of Formosa had come up overnight. She had to go with Zárate, a biologist from the Institute of Experimental Medicine she'd never met, who was joining the rabbit project.

Leaving the city was always bittersweet. She relished getting a bit of distance from her surroundings: it helped her re-evaluate the day-to-day. On the other hand, giving up the coherence of her habits made her feel somewhat uncomfortable. With her hands still wet, she stood motionless. Silent in thought. That's how her six-year-old son found her. One of its ears is falling off, he said, holding up a toy dog made from coarse fabric. It had an oval-shaped head – disproportionally oval – and its eyes, two translucent balls, were set far too high, where the forehead should have been. Marina Kezelman hunted for the sewing basket. She chose a strong thread and a slender needle and painstakingly began to sew. Just as she faced everything else in her life. Resolute. Relentless.

He woke up late, ten minutes after eleven, very unusual. He had toast spread with honey for breakfast. In his throat and at the top of his lungs – right in the hollows of the alveoli – he felt the need for a cigarette. He imagined – and for a moment he saw the scene in sharp detail – the bronchial tubes like a disputed territory, a war zone. The Gaza Strip in the middle of his chest.

He took a shower, hoping that the water might restore his sense of well-being. It was the right decision. He stepped out of the bathroom smelling of coconut soap and filled with a powerful rush of urgency: he had to crack on with the day, act fast, make decisions. Time was of the essence. Any delay would mean a critical waste. He had to get on with something, although he wasn't sure what. The anxiety was backfiring. His performance dropped to zero.

At 2 p.m. he opened his laptop. He pressed the ON button and waited for the operating system to initiate. The living room curtains rippled before him. It was Tuesday and the sun was barely grazing the edge of the planet. A certain splendour, almost a shimmer, emanated from earthly matter. That afternoon, the world was translucent, barely flickering. On his desk – it'd been exactly a week since he'd polished it – were three objects: a miniature horse, a postcard with a Chinese engraving and an adjustable lamp. Amer checked his emails. He deleted some spam and audited the personal messages. He paused on one from the National History Museum of La Plata. When he opened it, the rhythm of his breathing shifted. Work, the mere mention of the word, foisted a new dynamic upon him. Now, suddenly, without rising from his chair, he was climbing a mountain. They were offering him the chance to head up a team of taxidermists. An elephant was on its way from Africa, loaded in the hold of a ship, inside an extremely high-tech cold chamber. There wasn't much time to organise everything and they were relying on him wholeheartedly, on his anatomic knowledge, on his aptitude with polyurethane. Two months earlier he had worked miracles on an antelope. Everyone knew about it.

Amer stroked his chin and considered smoking. For fifteen seconds, he was lost in thought. The cigarette was a powerful, indispensable link in the chain. Without tobacco, he was half a man. He stood up abruptly and went towards the bathroom. Determined, he opened the medicine cabinet and pulled out a box of Xanax. He swallowed a pill, coaxing it down his throat with the water he drank straight from the tap, bent over the sink. He returned to the computer in a different mood, but now his mind was elsewhere. He googled brown bears. He browsed until he came across an article in the Spanish newspaper *El Mundo*. In 2015, a 180-kilo bear had killed three farmers in a small village in Asturias. We are not animals, said Amer, staring at the screen. The article included an image of a bear – apparently the culprit – standing upright on two legs. Its head was like a planet: huge, round and tilted slightly to the side, with two small ears towards the back, pricked up in alertness.

Blood does not have a price, read the German. He was waiting for his turn at a haemotherapy clinic. A friend of Marina Kezelman's was seriously ill and needed blood donors. Karl was certainly fit, but it was his height that had made everyone – within his universe of acquaintances, within his herd – deem him the man for the job. The German has to donate blood, they all agreed. They mistook size for health. Now Karl was biting the nail of his middle finger in a room lined with tiles. The process went like this: nurse, bed, needle, vein. Enduring the commotion of the drainage, the plasma on the cannula, speed and stillness at the same time. A circuit in which the German played an essential role without feeling responsible for it. There was something endless about the fluid streaming out of his body. That emptying-out held a meaning for him. His body understood it. He had become a shifting cartography, a stampede that bore witness, more than anything else, to his status as a foreigner.

They removed the needle – it made a sucking sound – and, taking his time, he gradually shifted upright. He stayed there sitting on the bed, his legs hanging ten centimetres from the floor. Silent. His face slack with perturbation. He was staring at a fixed point, a crack in the wall, the mark left by a nail or pin. In that instant, this blemish represented stability for Karl. It expressed certitude, permanence. The rest of the world, ceaselessly shifting, with its incessant movement, was not to be trusted; it introduced values of mutability. Despite everything – his own unsteadiness and that of his surroundings – he was determined to make an effort: he tried to stand up.

His legs gave way in the attempt and he collapsed, face first. He had fainted. As he went down, he took with him a metal table full of medical supplies. This caused as much noise as it did mess, and attracted the attention of the staff.

It took several people to lift him. The help was effective and he came round quickly. He was made to sit down in the waiting room. A nurse said to him: You're not going anywhere. Faced with Karl's silence, she asked: Do you understand what I'm saying?

After seven minutes, the German took a deep breath. He stood up and left the clinic without a word to anyone. He walked a few blocks with his mind blank, empty of images. The fresh air filled him with a sudden serenity and he felt clear-headed, free. Soon enough he arrived at a plaza. He headed down a path until he found a bench ringed by bushes. He sat in the same position, half-turned to the left, until a group of children took over the playground. At that moment, he felt certain that the past had expired. He thought about his son, about Marina Kezelman and about everything that the present revealed to him.

That same day, he organised things so he could return to the plaza with Simón. He sat on the same bench, though by now the sun was barely a gleam. Simón was a bit lost. He picked things off the ground, turning them over for a few seconds and then discarding them. Then he went over to the play equipment. He launched himself down the slide three times, but when another kid his age approached, he moved away and went looking for his father. He was bored, he said; he wanted to go home. The German straightened the collar of his shirt and briefly felt disheartened. He had brought a bag of sweets and a Frisbee. They played with the disc in the open space, a bit of rough grass next to the bandstand. The Frisbee came and went through the air. Simón threw it hard and upwards, creating a perfect ellipsis. As usual, though, his confidence got the better of him. He threw the disc forwards, straight towards Karl, whose good reflexes helped him dodge it just in time. It barely scraped his cheek. Five centimetres to the left and it would have got him straight in the eye.

Marina Kezelman got to the airport at 6:45 a.m. Her only piece of luggage was a small rucksack that she carried on her shoulder. She sat at a table in the café on the first floor and ordered a macchiato and an oat muffin. By the river bank, the reflection of the morning light – a lustrous sparkle – slid across the water. There were three fishermen standing next to a gas cylinder with a single burner on top. They rubbed their hands and sucked on the straws of their mate gourds. Every once in a while, with unnecessary rigour, they checked the tension on the fishing lines sunk invisibly into the river. All three men were large, almost fat, with short arms. They were wrapped in more layers of clothing than the temperature really warranted. The tallest one was wearing a grey turtleneck jumper that was too big for him. He spoke to his fellows, waving his arms above his head as if giving orders. Marina Kezelman stared at him. She felt that his presence destroyed the composition of the image; then, that a person like that couldn't fit into any kind of image. Marina Kezelman took a bite of her muffin. The taste instantly erased the fishermen, the landscape with the stove and even the river itself. Her gaze drifted for ten seconds as she savoured the muffin, until out of the blue she decided to send a WhatsApp to Zárate. I'll be there in ten, he replied right away.

Marina had received very precise descriptions of her companion: prominent jaw, short hair, small eyes. She recognised him as he went through the boarding queue. By way of introduction, the biologist extended his hand and gave his surname. He tripped over himself trying to explain the reason for his delay. His professional brilliance clashed with his expressive awkwardness. After some digression, it transpired that a neighbour's dog had bitten his eight-year-old daughter the night before. The animal, a young border collie, was usually calm, but the girl had goaded it into reacting. The dog seized her hand in its jaws and wouldn't let go. He'd had the fright of his life. They rushed to A&E. She got twelve stitches. To cut a long story short, Zárate hadn't slept a wink all night and when the alarm went off, he'd switched it off without realising. He swore again and again that he was usually a punctual guy. Marina Kezelman noticed a minor detail: the collar of his shirt was frayed. She guessed he was a person who didn't pay much heed to his appearance. She smiled. That detail – the worn-out fold of material – helped her intuit Zárate's vulnerability. A sensitive soul, she told herself.

The journey went smoothly. The noise of the engines filled the cabin like a negative echo and seeped into the passengers. The effect was a heavy lethargy. Marina Kezelman and Zárate only exchanged a few words before falling asleep. The biologist was so deeply asleep that he didn't even stir when the steward offered the breakfast tray. A government employee was waiting for them in Formosa. He was bony and straight-nosed and had brought a pick-up loaded with measuring equipment. Kezelman and Zárate let themselves be driven. They had barely twenty minutes to drop their things at the hotel. They'd been warned: the trip had to be productive. They drank coffee in the reception and left for the forest. They worked among the trees for four hours straight. They set hygrometers, exchanged data and figures, looked for rabbit warrens. The employee – whose name they never learned – waited for them in the van with the radio on. Late in the day, they returned via a rough track without saying a word. The driver didn't speak much, and they were exhausted. Once back at the hotel, they found out that their colleagues from the local government were inviting them out for dinner. They met in the lobby after a quick shower. Zárate had combed his hair to the back, and was wearing a sand-coloured polo neck. Marina Kezelman was wearing the same clothes. She regretted travelling so lightly.

Clara didn't show up at the second Tobar García meeting. Amer waited for her in vain. When the session was over, he told the guy from Córdoba that he wasn't heading back home. He made up an excuse. He meandered aimlessly for almost two hours and, close to midnight, stepped into a diner for a *milanesa*. He reassured himself with the thought that he would see Clara at the next meeting, but the following Tuesday, she didn't show up again. Amer felt like he'd died. Cigarettes tantalised him more than ever, but he resisted. Missing someone he didn't even know – he had exchanged twenty words with Clara, if that – was absurd, and he knew it, but this didn't stop him from suffering. He doubled his Xanax intake. Those two weeks were unbearable. When the third week came, Amer gave himself one final chance at the hospital. When he entered the room and saw her, he thought it was a mirage. Clara was sitting next to a pillar, absent, looking slightly fed up with life. Amer felt his blood run faster through his veins, his heart caught in his throat. He was struck by the realisation that being imaginative and being happy were one and the same. He ventured some idiotic phrase to ask Clara out. She stared at him as if he were speaking a different language.

They met up in San Telmo at a time that allowed them to circumvent the need for coffee or alcohol; they didn't want excuses to smoke. They walked down Defensa Street as far as Brazil Avenue, crossing the park into Barracas. There, Clara became more sociable. Amer asked her about her family. She was silent until suddenly, as if on a whim, she started telling him the story of an aunt from Trelew – her mother's sister – who'd had a urinary infection and almost died. Clara's voice was characterless, oiled by the least possible lubrication; a voice unaccustomed to uttering words. At the corner of Martín García, they bought mandarins and returned to the park to eat them. They sat on the grass with the roar of the traffic as a backdrop. The river floated in the air as if it were no more than wet earth. A dog struggled its way up the slope, noticed them and came over for a sniff. Perhaps because the dog reminded him of his work, Amer started talking about taxidermy. Clara listened to him with her gaze fixed on some distant point. She turned her head to look at him when he defined his profession as a philosophy of life. Amer said he created habitat dioramas for museums. He took a deep breath. With a certain pride he told her he was embalming an elephant for the National History Museum of La Plata. He slipped in that he was managing a big team. Clara nodded. She began to fix her hair with her large hands, which seemed neither strong, nor skilful, nor sensitive; she used them as if they were tools.

Karl spent all morning on a passage by Schumann. At 12:10 p.m. he placed the oboe on its stand. Outside, a brutal storm was sweeping everything before it: people, stunted trees. The German felt safe inside his four walls. He took a deep breath and went into the kitchen. Despite it being the middle of the day, he had to switch on the light. A faint bluish gleam filtered through the skylight. He cut a slice of bread, spread some hummus on it and jammed it into his mouth. He was desperately hungry; his struggle with the music hit him right in the stomach. Surviving the frustration was key, and food always helped. Marina Kezelman was away. Simón would get back from school in about half an hour. Karl cracked on with lunch. Pasta with cream, a dish he knew his son would appreciate. While he waited for the water to boil, the German reflected on his sense of living only a half present: every one of his actions seemed incomplete. He felt debilitated by a future nostalgia.

Simón got home at the usual time. He dropped his school bag onto a chair and went to the bathroom to wash his hands. The seam of his uniform had come undone, and he didn't have much to say. Mistaking his standoffishness for despondency, Karl asked him if something had happened at school, but the boy shook his head. Once he'd finished eating – he wolfed everything down in a rush – Simón stood up and walked to the window. He observed a whirlpool of wind and leaves and a black chunk of sky. He moved his lips like in a whisper. From behind, Karl's son looked younger. His dishevelled hair, his narrow back, his feeble nape. Standing at the glass, inches from the storm, his fragility doubled. Simón was the reverse of the world. His father was doing the dishes, wearing a chequered apron over a burgundy shirt. Once he'd put everything away in the cupboards, he took out a box of Lindt chocolates. He gave one to Simón. The boy unwrapped it and greedily stuffed it into his mouth. Thunder roared outside. Simón, chewing silently, tried to translate his thoughts. He stayed like that for a while until he decided to talk. When he did, his voice sounded two octaves beneath his normal register. I don't feel well, I think I've got a temperature. Karl touched his forehead and immediately went in search of the thermometer. It wasn't easy to find: it was inside a pencil box on Marina Kezelman's desk.

The thermometer marked 36.7 °C. Nevertheless, Karl sent his son to bed and laid a wet flannel over his forehead. He stayed there until the boy fell asleep, holding the toy dog Marina had given him. Karl sat in the dark for a while, very close to his son. It was night-time in the middle of the day. His eyes got used to the lack of light and he realised that – by chance – he was staring fixedly at the toy in his son's arms. It seemed to him that in that toy, somehow, the unknown and the familiar were unexpectedly combined.

Marina Kezelman and Zárate waited at the door of the hotel. The night refined them, polishing their features, turning them sharp and beautiful. Their faces looked like portraits by El Greco. They talked about banal things: TV series, tourism, sport. They glanced at their phones out of the corners of their eyes, as if it were a duty. Neither of them was partial to the cold, but they were grateful for the four-degree temperature drop. I forgot my shawl, she said.

At the agreed time, the same guy came to fetch them in the same van. The trip lasted exactly eight minutes. This time, Zárate – calm and clean – decided to be more sociable. He asked the driver what his name was, and proceeded to include him in the conversation. The guy raised his eyebrows. He was cautious, as if his words were being taken as evidence in a trial. His name was Juan. He had been born in a town near Quito and he'd emigrated to Argentina not long before. Marina Kezelman said: You can't really tell you're not from round here. Her phone rang right after her remark. It was Karl. Simón hadn't been feeling well, he'd been somewhat ill. What do you mean, somewhat ill? she yelled. Karl replied and Marina Kezelman hung up without saying goodbye. The German was always putting his foot in it. Malapropos: that was the word for him.

The hosts were a pair of civil servants: the woman was an engineer and the man a lawyer. They met at the best steak restaurant in town, a vast place with rustic décor. Traditional songs played in the background. The ambience of the get-together was relaxed from the outset. A sommelier wearing a tight suit and sporting a tiny moustache presented them with the wine list. They drank parsimoniously from large glasses, adjusting quickly to the situation. Each movement fastened to the one that followed; they were carried along on an undulating wave of comfort. They inhabited a present that was weightless, fickle even, and yet at the same time effortlessly assembled; it was the very embodiment of something sound, something firm and tangible: a space of utter certainty. They felt they'd known each other forever. That was the temperature of the evening. The meat – tender, cooked to perfection – was another element in this equilibrium. It appeared on a cast iron griddle pan. Marina Kezelman ordered a tonic water to alternate with the wine, and they brought her a Schweppes in a miniature ice bucket. A nice detail, she thought.

They finished well after midnight. There was hardly any movement in the street. Occasionally a car would appear, but it would pass without urgency, trailing drowsiness in its wake. Everything was translucent, crystal clear. The night echoed over the landscape: the animals, the wind in the trees, and all that rich and compact mass of grassland. Marina Kezelman and Zárate bid farewell to their companions as if they were old friends. There were promises of future encounters and slaps on the back, all four of them following the rites of sociability to a T. Marina Kezelman and Zárate climbed into the van through the same door and began their journey back. For both, the car felt like an observatory. They dissolved into their thoughts as they were driven in silence. On the other side of the glass, the city – a colony of dormant buildings – was well-defined and alien. They reached the hotel in a blink of an eye. The concierge – whose face was smooth and hairless – told them the bar was still open and gestured for them to make the most of their complimentary welcome drink. Marina Kezelman ordered a Campari, Zárate, a gin and tonic. They talked about the research institute they had in common and told stories from university. Zárate, emboldened and slightly nostalgic, placed his elbows on the table. He ordered a second round of drinks, but the bar had just closed. Marina Kezelman took the opportunity to withdraw. The light from above accentuated her cheekbones. It was clearly time to call it a night. They had to get up early: the return flight left at 7:12 a.m.

They stepped into the lift. Their rooms were both on the third floor. They took twenty steps down the corridor and, when the moment came to say goodnight, the shift occurred, the change that they had both anticipated. There was a brush between them, the slightest graze that served them both − in the same instant − as proof, and precisely because they couldn't ignore the force of the truth contained in this apparent insignificance, they had to act on it. Their hands touched first, then their lips. There were no words, nor was there time to take in all the details that would make an eternal image of the scene. In haste, tangled, furtive, they made their way into Zárate's room. He stumbled. Then it was all a frenzied rolling on the bed that left them gasping for air. They halted to sip water from a small bottle. They walked to the window and looked out. The street was deserted; this place belonged to no one. They ended up on the floor. The back of her head against a corner of the wall. He on top of her, exhausted, with a rash on his neck. They slept wrapped in the quilt and left for the airport together. They were united by a certain look: they both wore black sunglasses of comparable design. On the plane, they talked about the future of the research project that had brought them together. Without admitting it to the other, they both saw the previous night's encounter as an isolated event, an exception, a mere product of their circumstances; something that would never happen again.

Clara wove her life together with simplicity. She didn't ponder, she went straight to the point. But this approach – healthily reductive – often left her bewildered and frustrated, two feelings associated with other aspects of her temper. The combination exuded a complex substance that generally took the form of guilt.

She was relentless with herself, and with the rest of the world too. She'd just turned thirty-six when she decided to become a PE teacher. At the time, she was working in a perfume shop in the district of Once and smoked a pack of Marlboro a day. The morning she signed up for the course, she quit smoking. Her boss had been the one who'd told her about the group meetings at the Tobar García hospital. And Clara – more out of obligation than eagerness – began to attend. Amer caught her eye from the get-go. And so he entered her life swiftly. It was unexpected, sudden. He altered her entire metabolism. Deftly, though, she managed to keep a balanced head, assimilating it all quicker than she'd imagined.

One weekend, a month after they'd started going out, they drove her Ford Galaxy to the national park at Costanera Sur. They walked down a path that grew steeper the closer it got to the river. Amer carried a bag over his shoulder. He had tried to think of everything: a blanket, biscuits, mate tea. The outing had put them both in a good mood, yet underneath that sense of well-being – or rather, at the same level of consciousness, like a sort of varnish that tainted their enthusiasm – they had the impression that they were playing parts in a scene that wasn't theirs. They chatted placidly. They jumped from one topic to the next until the dialogue very gradually narrowed down to films. A few weeks earlier, Amer had walked out of a cinema fifteen minutes into the movie. It was something that had never happened to him before: the main character was so much like him that the film had become unbearable to watch. The resemblance wasn't physical; it was about how the character related to his life, the questions he asked himself, his ambivalence. You're crazy. I wouldn't go to the movies with you even if they paid me, said Clara with a forced smile. Just then, she was distracted by a brightly coloured bird perched on a branch. It opened its wings and folded them again. Its nervous eyes darted over its surroundings. Three seconds passed. Then it took off, flying low. The sun hit the ground and made it weightless.

Clara and Amer found some shade near the shore. A hermetic kind of smell rose from the river: it was the air getting moist and then returning to the atmosphere. A light breeze ruffled Clara's hair and two or three locks fell across her face. Amer had undone the buttons on his shirt, revealing intensely white and freckled skin. The day was pristine. The sky emerged from the brim of the earth. Everything seemed crisp and clear. Things reverberated: bodies, weeds, detritus.

The afternoon shot past like lightning. At 3 p.m. countless sailing boats gathered on the horizon, attracting everyone's attention. A woman with fat arms dipped her feet in the water. Slowly, she went further in through the rocks, feeling her way, searching carefully for where to step. She made a gesture – a wave to the sun – and returned to her group, a family of four. They playing music and talking loudly. They had everything they needed: bread, ham, beers, plenty of Coca-Cola. Her husband was wearing a cap that read 'John Deere'. There were two kids between six and eight. The oldest got on well with Amer right away. They kicked a ball around for a while, going from one side of the beach to the other. When they got tired, each of them went their own way.

Amer lay down next to Clara to catch his breath. Enveloped in the late afternoon glare, they played a game of *truco*. They took it way too seriously. Absurd as it may seem, the prospect of defeat was tragic to them. The air cooled to ice in the tension of the scene. This meant that, as soon as they disagreed on something, an argument broke out. Truth be told, they were quarrelling over nothing. After a while, Amer took a deep breath, held the air in his lungs and let it out. He opted for peace, but Clara chose to pursue her indignation. The landscape and the afternoon evaporated. She wasn't going to give in, that much was clear. In fact, she stood up, folded the blanket and packed up everything; she was ready to leave.

Eventually they buried the hatchet. It was a titanic task. They made it to the Galaxy dragging their feet, sapped of energy. Clara dropped Amer off at the corner of Paseo Colón and Corrientes. She kissed him quickly on the cheek and drove off. A second later, he was a blank soul in the traffic. He went into a pizzeria and ordered a beer and three empanadas. He bolted them down as if he hadn't had a bite to eat in months. Then he went home on the subway and slept through till morning. When he woke up, his temples were throbbing. From then on, he would avoid confrontation with Clara at all costs. The argument had set a precedent.

One morning Karl decided to paint the living room. He held Simón's hand as they walked to school. He left him at the gate and headed to a café to kill time. He ordered a coffee from a waiter who looked just like Samuel Beckett. Then he focused on the people filing in and out of the subway. It was hardly an unfamiliar scene, but this time the experience felt strange. For some reason, he felt that he'd never been part of such a vast collective, neither in Argentina nor in Germany. He slipped his glasses on and, like any other native of Buenos Aires, leafed through the newspaper that'd been left on the table next to him. He skimmed the articles. They were all variations on the same thing. He stopped to read the adverts for home appliances. He dedicated several minutes to this. Following that, he looked up at the ceiling and wondered how he might look, there and then, to everyone else: next to the window, an empty cup in front of him, dishevelled hair and glasses. He was sure that this image didn't represent who he really was. He started to entertain himself imagining he was someone else, anyone else; someone from the Flores neighbourhood who'd never even heard of the Brandenburg Gate, for instance.

At 9:10 a.m. he went into the paint shop. They'd had some damp on a wall and that problem was now sorted, but he was eager to repaint the stained plaster. In that stain, Karl saw the profile of a woman – sharp nose, broad forehead – that reminded him of the one who'd brought him up in Munich. He bought two litres of emulsion, sealant, sandpaper, rollers and a synthetic brush. He started working at ten on the dot. He prepared things carefully.

He covered the floor with newspapers and the furniture with plastic sheeting. Following the instructions, he sanded the wall first. By the time he'd finished, the dust had even got under his nails. He brushed it off as best he could and went to the kitchen for some water. His throat was dry. He opened the fridge and saw four one-litre bottles of Heineken lying on the shelves. He'd bought them a day earlier, and now they were cold. The decision came swiftly. He poured himself a glass and gulped it down in one. He immediately refilled it and, once again, guzzled it down. He returned to the living room with the third glass full. He spent until noon cleaning the walls with paint remover and listening to classical music on the radio. During that time, he made four trips to the kitchen. He drank two litres of beer without even realising.

Simón got back from school and Karl cooked some chicken. While he was preparing the ingredients, he was hit by a terrible bout of indigestion and paused the beer. They drank water with lunch. By 3 p.m., he'd forgotten his discomfort and had opened the third bottle of beer; before half past, the fourth. All of a sudden, he felt a kind of torpor in his head – a pressure on his temples – but he attributed it to the smell of the paint thinner instead of the alcohol. He decided he should abandon the task until the following day. He didn't want to intoxicate himself. Right away, responding to his zeal for productivity, he started playing the oboe. He stopped to send a WhatsApp message to his wife. He described in detail how the painting had gone. Then he returned to the oboe and, as he tried to strike a high note, something very odd happened: one of his teeth – the lateral incisor – came loose. He rushed to the bathroom to check and indeed, that was exactly what had happened. From then on, he couldn't stop probing it with his tongue; he kept pushing it backwards, relishing the pain. He lay down on the bed to focus on this sole task, but he didn't last long: two minutes later, he was asleep. Sound asleep, face up. Simón, who from his bedroom had been following his dad's activities by the sounds he made, was surprised by the sudden silence and came out to have a look. He stared at Karl for a while. His father was huge, a giant who wore size 46 shoes. A faint, barely visible vapour emerged from his open mouth, accompanied by a mechanical sound, like the grinding of cogs.

Everything began to make sense. At 8 a.m., Marina Kezelman was rustling up breakfast for her son when she saw a very orderly line of ants descending from the granite worktop towards a hole in the wall at skirting board level, a crack barely visible to the naked eye. The poison hadn't worked. It seemed the nest was now elsewhere. She took a glass of chocolate milk and a plate of sponge biscuits to the living room.

She paused to watch Simón, who was chewing slowly, and for two minutes she freed herself from a feeling she'd been carrying for a while. Fear or distress; she wasn't sure which. Kezelman was wearing her hair straighter than usual, down to her shoulders. A week earlier she'd gone to the hairdresser's. She'd wanted to look presentable for her fortieth birthday, which they'd celebrated in a restaurant by the river. They went to bed after 6 a.m. and made use of the orange vibrator, with excellent results. But afterwards Marina Kezelman couldn't get to sleep. A stream of images paraded through her brain, keeping her half-awake, until she decided to get up. She blamed the morning traffic for her sleeplessness.

When Simón finished drinking his chocolate milk, Marina Kezelman took the dishes to the kitchen, washed everything up and got herself into the shower. Wrapped in a towel and wearing poorly fitting flip-flops, she had a moment of clarity: she had to get rid of the ant infestation at all costs. She searched online for a pest control company and hired their services without asking any questions. They showed up at 7:45 a.m. the following day, carrying sophisticated-looking equipment.

Two young men, who looked as if they'd just emerged from puberty, investigated every nook and cranny. They would stop periodically to whisper to each other, as if they were tackling an extremely serious, extraordinary case. They were done within an hour. They handed over a leaflet with detailed information about the low-toxicity products they'd used; they were committed to protecting the environment. In actual fact, more than anything else, this was a communication strategy by the company they worked for, a carefully planned way to promote a more favourable corporate image.

Once she was alone, Kezelman sat on the living room sofa with a can of Sprite. She inhaled the neutral smell of the poison and felt like a stranger in her own home. She rested her head against the back of the sofa, closed her eyes and tried hard to apply a meditation technique she'd learnt when she was twenty-five, but to no avail. The usual happened: she got distracted. Her mind was elsewhere. In an hour's time, she was supposed to give an update on the project to her supervisor. At that precise moment, her phone rang. She jumped as if she'd never heard a sound like it in her entire life.

Thursday dawned glorious but clouded over as evening approached. Clara and Amer had agreed to meet in San Telmo at 8 p.m. They wanted to go to a legendary cocktail bar where Negronis were prepared with Tanqueray gin and Italian vermouth. Four hours before they were supposed to meet, Amer left the museum – earlier than expected – feeling deeply disappointed. After a series of postponements, he'd been informed that the elephant job had fallen through. The port authorities had stopped the specimen from being unloaded. Their reasons were irrefutable. The preservation chamber had been affected by a fault on the open sea – something to do with an unstable thermostat – and the body had begun to decompose. Amer heard the news and flew into a rage. He turned pale and the veins on his neck stood out. I'm going to faint, he thought. Twenty seconds later, once he'd recovered, he banged a fist on the desk. What kind of person doesn't keep his word? he shouted at the director. He'd never been this keen on a job before. More than the money, he'd yearned for the prestige. When he met up with Clara, he made no reference to the matter. Her presence somehow made it all seem less important.

They spent some time strolling through the neighbourhood, walking for five or six blocks. They looked at antiques: jars, salt shakers, picture frames. The couple's mood circled over the morass of trinkets. Even the most inert object, something usually discarded, was in transit here, and presented itself as faintly iridescent. At the corner of Chile and Bolívar, they heard salsa music and got a whiff of fried food. These details made them change their plans. They gave up on the idea of the cocktail place and just went into the first bar they found.

They climbed a narrow set of steps and sat on a sofa in the corner. They both ordered Campari with orange juice, then switched to something else. They browsed through the menu and made their decisions according to names rather than ingredients. They stayed for three hours, spread-eagled over patterned cushions, their emotions so volatile – a current that coursed through their bodies from head to toe – that they felt exceptional somehow, even irreplaceable in each other's lives. The scent of the night – its honeyed exhalations – gradually cut them out as if they were made of paper, and plunged them into a dialogue that felt austere and sharp-edged. They talked about dead stars, black holes and the value of keeping fit. Amer said he had a nephew who weighed his food on a set of scales before eating it. He was a bodybuilder. He only drank imported products: peanut tea, Evian water, raw cabbage juice. Clara was listening but from 5000 miles away, not looking at him. They were both tipsy, though still far from the point of collapse.

Clara hadn't brought her car in order to be able to drink, so as soon as they got a bit cold, they called an Uber. A white Toyota came to pick them up. Neither of them saw what they were experiencing as especially significant. They went to Amer's house. It was the second night they were spending together. At one point, while they were making love, Amer had a moment of bewilderment: he completely forgot who he was with. He tried to hide his confusion as best he could. They fell asleep under a thin sheet. The cold air made them reach for each other.

They drank mate in the morning. Clara was wearing some of his clothes. It wasn't winter but they fancied the idea of keeping each other warm. They faced one another across a folding table in the kitchen. The glare of the day reverberated through an aluminium-framed window. You snored all night, she said as if announcing something serious. Amer shifted in his chair. At first he denied it, but after ten seconds he admitted: My tongue muscles are a bit loose. Clara shook her head in resignation and said, I can't believe this is the time I've chosen to quit smoking. It is what it is, he said. They heard the muffled sound of footsteps. The upstairs neighbours. They're considerate like that, said Amer, they tip-toe around the flat. It'll be hard to sleep with you, sweetheart, said Clara, the snoring sounds come from your chest. It's as if something is scratching you. Amer swallowed a morsel. Snoring helps get the nasty stuff out, it expels all the crap from your body, he said.

Clara also changed position – and subject. She talked about life after her separation. Damned blessed happiness, she said. Amer put the kettle on again to prepare some more mate. They say beekeeping is good for reducing stress, Clara remarked. Amer felt as if he were watching a performance, but this impression didn't weaken Clara's words. She was silent for a few seconds.

Karl was waiting for his entry. His attention was trained on a single point. The oboe's mouthpiece between his lips, his fingers on the keys. The light – a solid stream from above – offered an excellent view of the score, the notes seeming to stand out in relief. It also had another effect: it flattened the German's features. The chessboard of his face was simplified to a handful of gestures: thin hair – stirred by the slightest breeze – above the mask of naked, lidless, lashless eyes, totally blank.

It was the fourth time they'd played the piece. The orchestra moved in waves. The musicians were playing with a kind of saturation that intensified the sound, making it thicker, more robust. So much so that it naturally cohered into a collective expression, joyful and indivisible. Karl had a solo to play. He kept botching his entry. On the fourth attempt – that is, the fourth time the entire orchestra repeated the piece – he overcame the hurdle and felt grateful to life. For this reason, and this reason alone, when the rehearsal was over, he did something very unusual for him: he stayed behind to drink mate with his colleagues. The trombonist, a grey-haired guy with long sideburns, was celebrating his birthday and had brought sweet pastries from a bakery on Corrientes Avenue. Karl had a bite of the Neapolitan *sfogliatella* and got so excited – he ate two – that as soon as he left the theatre, he called his wife and told her about the whole experience. Marina Kezelman barely paid attention to his story. She held the phone between her shoulder and ear so she could carry on typing on her laptop as Karl talked. The German could hear the clicking of the keys.

I'm swamped with work, said Kezelman. I have fifty emails to reply to. The conversation ended abruptly, almost without a goodbye. Karl hesitated for a moment. He wasn't usually inclined to press for definitions, but the matter lingered in his mind for a while. An hour later, when his foot touched the subway platform, he was still thinking about it. What he'd just felt – the pleasure of the *sfogliatella* – had faded. It had found no echo in the only person who could confirm the value of his experience.

He let one subway train go by and bought a box of chocolate-coated peanuts. He sat on a bench, placing the oboe case between his legs, and began to eat them one by one. Understanding and resignation grew inside him, slowly, with each pearl of chocolate. Argentina was the perfect antithesis to Germany, with all the pros and cons that this entailed. For the second time that day, a childhood dream popped into his head. To stop the images from crystallising, he stood up and started walking towards the turnstiles. A teenager in shorts and a blue t-shirt crossed the scene. A government official was making a speech on the TV screens suspended from the ceiling. The voice was an electric reverberation, unintelligible. Karl paced, trying to adjust the way his shirt sat on his shoulders. He stopped to look at a map of the subway network. He read the names of the stations one by one: Tronador, Lacroze, Dorrego. They were empty words to him, words reduced to sound, pure acoustic effect.

Two minutes later, the train arrived. Karl sat with his back to the window and withdrew from the everyday. Unwittingly, he found a means to disengage: the clatter submerged him in an unexpected experience of *satori*. Suddenly, the German found himself clasped to a present that materialised and disintegrated in the same instant.

At Pueyrredón station, he plugged his headphones into his mobile and listened to music that resembled

Ravel but wasn't. And so he stayed until he reached 9 de Julio: his stop. Exiting the train, he'd taken three steps on the platform, no more than three, when a fifteen-stone man in a grey suit walked into him. The collision was gradual. Their shoes struck first, then their bodies. An accident, a classic act of clumsiness. The sensible response would have been to let life carry on as usual, but things went awry from the outset. Rage spiked not because of the intensity of the impact, but because both men stared daggers at each other. Clearly, this was a duel. The other guy, around forty years old, lawyer-faced, was the first to shoot. A spiteful diatribe sprang from his mouth. You fucking clumsy asshole, he said. And he repeated: You fucking clumsy asshole. It sounded as if he were reading from a script.

The German took a deep breath. He placed the oboe case on the floor, laid his headphones on top of it and got ready to charge. He raised his head and added an inch to his already imposing height. What ensued was the fight, its chaos. And yet the remarkable thing, what was truly remarkable, was the structure amid that glorious anarchy. First came a prologue of shoves and challenges, then, slaps. The two men fused together in a ferocious embrace that left both of them breathless. It was a clash of titans. They bent like branches – their bones adjusting to the new shapes – until, entangled, they fell to the ground, intent on struggling to the death.

They hit each other wherever they could: stomach, arms, face. They kicked, bit, strangled. They had more than enough time to cause damage. In the frenzy, they rolled into a wall and stayed there, bunched up and immobile, until the police came and pulled them apart. For dignity's sake, they pretended they wanted to carry on; in truth, they were exhausted. The suit lapel of the lawyer-faced guy was torn and he was bleeding from his mouth. Of the two men, he looked the worse for wear. Someone passed Karl his glasses. One of the arms was gone. He folded them up and robotically stuck them into one of his pockets. The rest was paperwork and reprimands, a police officer jotting down details and talking over his radio. With that, the adversaries parted, strangers once more.

Karl practically crawled home, dragging his oboe. The house was empty. He stepped into the shower and stayed almost an hour under the water. Then he wrapped himself in a robe and lay down on the living room sofa. He pictured his German daughter crossing the street and felt a lump in his throat. In that instant, he realised there wasn't a single part of his body that didn't hurt. It even hurt to breathe. He curled up on his side, aching for relief. He rested his head on a cushion and closed his eyes.

Marina Kezelman looked at her phone screen light up. A rush of exhilaration flooded her chest; out of sheer excitement, she took a sip of Sprite. Only then did she answer. She jumped to her feet at the sound of Zárate's voice. She walked to the window and drew back the curtains with one swift gesture. Eagerness altered the tone of her voice.

At the other end of the line, Zárate was acting a part: the experienced guy. He toyed with his pauses, made a joke every now and then. He insinuated that there was nothing important enough to worry him. For every unforeseen event, he had a strategy. He'd reached the degree zero of fortuitousness. He invited Kezelman out for a drink. The invitation sounded like a minor detail in the course of the conversation. Today, he said. They agreed to meet at 7 p.m. at a place in Palermo. At 7 p.m. then, she confirmed. The idea was to have a few drinks, but if things led that way, the bar also offered good food. An aperitif is always a crossroads. Without a doubt, said Zárate, noting the bombast of his own expression.

Marina Kezelman arrived early and made the most of her time alone to wander the neighbourhood. She paused in front of random shop displays that caught her eye. She crossed El Salvador Street and passed the open window of a house, the sound of the TV news filtering outside. She brushed a hand across her forehead as if she'd remembered something or wanted to erase a worry. The evening light – a persistent glow – turned her hair a shade lighter. She dug into her handbag and pulled out her phone. She called Karl and lied with total spontaneity, as if it were easy for her. I have a meeting with the research team, she said. It'll go on till late, she added. Then the whole group is going out for something to eat. She made sure to remind him that there were veggie burgers in the freezer for him and Simón. She hung up with an extraordinary feeling of relief. She breathed in through her nostrils and exhaled slowly. She was determined to enjoy the night.

Zárate arrived at seven on the dot. They went for a table on the terrace and ordered beer. Every now and then, their hands would touch accidentally, and this casual contact jolted them back to the intimacy they'd shared. When it comes to animals, everyone thinks they know all there is to know, said Zárate, mentioning an article by Skinner on behaviourism in everyday life. Intermittently, like a nervous tic, he'd touch his nose with his middle finger as if adjusting a pair of invisible glasses. He spoke freely, gesticulating with gusto. Marina Kezelman thought that the man in front of her – so kind and enthusiastic – was different to the one she'd seen for the first time at the airport, almost his opposite. She also told herself – not without pride – that this change was her doing: her femininity had forged a new man, someone capable of sidestepping trivial matters without abandoning them altogether. Kezelman brushed a fingertip against her blouse and the contact with the silk made her shiver. At that moment, almost rudely, she interrupted Zárate. Hold it there for a second, she said, I have to nip to the toilet. Suddenly, she noticed a shift in herself as well: she'd just unveiled a new personality. She was in charge.

She returned with damp hands. Zárate welcomed her back with a smile, as if she was returning from a long trip. I missed you, he said. Marina Kezelman ignored the stupid line as best she could and, from that moment on, the pace of the encounter was different. The first part had transpired in slow motion, with graceful placidity. This second sequence, meanwhile, was electric. Kezelman and Zárate were sprinters in a 100-metre race. Perfect and luminous. They ordered salmon gravlax to share, and a bottle of Chablis. The plate was set in the middle of the table, the wine in a cooler. From one moment to the next, their eagerness and the alcohol did away with their surroundings altogether. The bar, the food and the people around them ceased to exist. Zárate braced his forearms on the table so as to get closer to Marina Kezelman, wanting to kiss her. Unfortunately, the table legs were unsteady and the whole thing began to wobble. Everything – fish, wine cooler, wine glasses – was on the verge of tumbling to the ground. Four lurching seconds. Kezelman was the first to overcome their paralysis. She stood to pick up a napkin, and as she sat down again, with a swift movement, she leant down to Zárate and brushed her lips against his. It was a fleeting touch, a slightly less than casual spark, which nonetheless foretold what they knew was going to happen. Above their heads, clinging to a wall marked by moisture stains, a bougainvillea fanned out its branches and somehow concealed the night.

Amer placed the otter's fur in a basin of water to soak. That was the first step. Then he had to salt it, tan it and oil it. Taxidermy is a time-consuming, painstaking process. The otter was a favour for a friend, not a paid job. He couldn't bring himself to say no. Outside, it was pouring with rain. It was noon on a Wednesday and the city had been brought to a standstill. Amer could hear the water gushing from the storm drains in the street. Everywhere was flooded, streaming with rubbish. Every now and then, a peal of thunder heralded the end of the world.

Amer went to the bathroom and washed his hands obsessively. Then he went to the kitchen, pulled the only remaining piece of bread out of a bag and ate it in a couple of dry bites. He opened the fridge and closed it again. He lay down on the living-room sofa to plan his future and consider some options. He stayed there for a while with his feet on the coffee table, longing for a smoke. Storms encouraged idleness, offered a time outside of time. Amer half-closed his eyes and sighed. The image of a grizzly bear standing on its hind legs flashed into his mind. He recalled the words of an English naturalist: if a bear associates a human with food, any attempt to scare it away or stop it from approaching will be unsuccessful. He smoothed his hair with his hand and leapt to his feet. He opened his laptop and searched for images of grizzly bears. Standing upright, drinking water, growling, peering over a cliff, with their cubs, dead, with a hunter's foot resting on their side, with a hunter's rifle jabbing into their back. Somehow, these huge bodies harboured opposites: sweetness or even vulnerability, ferociousness or invincibility. There was something about such animals – a cypher, a quiddity – that led Amer to a wellspring of meanings. This self-evident truth lost its clarity, however, when he tried to give it a name. There was no way of putting it into words. In Amer's eyes, it was precisely this elusive element that made bears such boundless, magnificent creatures.

Something sudden, an unexpected craving. He grabbed his phone, dialled the number of an ice-cream shop and ordered half a litre of salted caramel to be delivered. They told him it'd be a while because of the rain, but in the end it showed up sooner than expected. He went to the kitchen, put the container in the freezer and saw the washbowl with the otter on the counter. He lowered it to the floor in two movements. As he was completing the second, he felt a sharp pull in his lower back: a spark, an electric shock, death, death itself. He stayed squatting on his heels until he could recover his strength. He hobbled into the bathroom, half buckled over. He groped in the medicine cabinet until he found a jar. He took a Paracetamol. It wasn't easy to force the pill down his throat. He drank water straight from the tap, then immediately made his way towards his bed, removed his shoes and lay down with great care. He wasn't quite horizontal; his upper back was propped against two pillows crammed into the bedstead. He turned his head and saw a cup with a bit of leftover tea on the bedside table. He drank it in one swig. He was thirsty and imagined the liquid – cold dregs – descending his throat and spreading through his interior. The tea permeated the tissues of his body, somehow restoring the spirit he thought he'd lost forever.

The remote control was in reach, so he switched on the television. A dermatologist was talking about honey, which apparently had become a valued ingredient in cosmetics. The face of a female model was now being shown in close-up. A face mask was being applied to her with a brush. Meanwhile, a voice-over recited the benefits of this natural product: enzymes, vitamins, nutrients. The pain and the Paracetamol had hollowed Amer's head into a cavern, and reality – at that very moment the doctor's words represented the synthesis of everything real – was filtering into this hole like an empty, unfathomable echo. An echo which, however absurd it might seem, spoke the truth, the most convincing, overwhelming, seemingly non-existent yet no less radical of truths. Clara was right, Amer suddenly said to himself: he had to pursue the apiculture project. It'd only been a passing remark, a trifle, but it had stayed with him. Apiculture, apiculture, he said again and again, like a mantra. And what he imagined wasn't a hobby, but the very opposite: a central activity around which all the events in his life would orbit – like planets, asteroids or cosmic rubbish – in a single, perfect ellipsis.

At 8 p.m., Karl stood up as best he could and went to the bathroom. He urinated in a long stream. He kept his eyes closed, pressing the palm of his hand into the wall. He looked for a painkiller, something, anything to make him feel better. He searched and searched but found nothing. At the bottom of one of the drawers, buried among plasters, hairclips and hairbands, he found a tattered blister pack of aspirin. He put two in his mouth. They were so bitter that he spat them right back out. He washed his face. As he dried it, he looked at his reflection in the mirror: swollen red eyes, busted lip, scraped forehead. A long cut across his chin. He didn't recognise himself. The distorted features had turned him into someone else. He thought that another hot shower would bring some relief, so he turned the tap on and let the water run. The bathroom quickly filled with steam. Still dressed, he sat with one buttock on the edge of the toilet, completely motionless. All of a sudden, he was unable to make even the feeblest effort. He had no energy, no will. He turned the tap off, left the bathroom with a towel around his shoulders and lay face down on the sofa.

Soon after he sent a message to his wife. The reply came forty minutes later via a recorded audio. Marina Kezelman was at a birthday party with Simón. The recording captured the background noise: screaming kids and some beats from a classic Stevie Wonder song, which entered Karl's head and zigzagged around inside. It followed him like a friendly rhythm for the next four hours. Somehow, this music – joyously melancholic, like an intimate memory – altered the German's emotional parabola, and allowed him to emerge, very gradually, from his state of almost total indifference. It was the only positive outcome of the exchange. Because the fact is that Kezelman hardly said anything at all, addressing him in a tone as utterly impersonal as a computer. We'll be late, the recording said. Don't wait for us. And with that, the conversation was over.

Karl was in the middle of the Sahara Desert and didn't know which direction to take. He hobbled to his bedroom. As the hours passed, his pain only intensified. He found more aspirin in the bedside table drawer and decided to try and take them. To make them easier to swallow, he dissolved them in water with sugar and drank the mix. It made no difference: he felt another pulse of nausea. He sat on the sofa to recover, leaning his head back. Something always happens to foreigners, he said out loud. Within his circle he'd heard stories that justified this thought. He imagined himself fulfilling a strict routine, much stricter than the one he currently maintained. He'd hoped that his own habits and those of his wife would have gradually converged after they moved in together, but they never had. Quite the opposite. He believed that this – the assimilation of habits – was critical to a person's wellbeing. He yawned and covered his mouth with one hand. In order to resist the void – something he knew very well – he needed an activity, an occupation that would save him from self-pity. He opened his laptop on the coffee table and checked the time. He counted hours. Then he called Germany via Skype. The first attempt failed. He'd wanted to talk to a cousin in Olching. He then tried a friend who lived in Berlin. This second effort was a success. He heard the click that opened the call and said: Dirk? Sound and image were slightly out of sync and the delay disrupted their communication. The chat felt distant. At points – especially during the first few minutes – it seemed like an exchange between two strangers. But it gradually deepened: they began talking about personal and family issues, albeit with a certain coldness that prevailed the entire time. Karl wanted to know something about Ebba, his daughter. Dirk instinctively avoided the question. Then, illuminated by a reflex from his inner *camera obscura*, he said: There are things that start by chance but never come to an end. Dirk – with his forehead of steel and the world's sharpest nose – took a deep breath.

One morning Ebba had had an accident. She was riding her bike through Büchnerweg Square and fell. She crashed into a flower bed. Between the surgery and the recovery, her life was on hold for a year. She was naturally a thoughtful soul, but her convalescence – her forced reclusion – had deepened this trait in her. There was no act, no matter how insignificant, that she didn't speculate about. This is how, as she thought and thought and thought some more, she'd come to understand that she had always repressed two crucial desires: to travel and to have pets. She concluded that true existence – wholehearted, full – was one that rejected stasis and relied on animal affection. As soon as she recovered, Ebba sold a few things, bought a Yorkshire terrier and embarked on a journey with no return date. She'd recently written to Dirk from a pet-friendly hotel in Harare. Karl listened to his friend talk about his daughter and felt as if he were discussing a total stranger. He fixed his eyes on the screen. On Dirk. Actually, on Dirk's mouth, which sometimes looked like a frayed purple thread; at others, a centrifugal spiral. He had the feeling that this story he'd just heard – a preposterous story, almost implausible – contained hidden clues that, if he could only decipher them properly, would prove useful to understanding his own life, or even to predicting it.

Marina Kezelman's heart thudded in her chest. They got out of the taxi and saw a man wearing flip-flops and tracksuit bottoms; he was going through the rubbish. No words, said Zárate. No words. He'd pulled up the lapels of his blazer. Every gesture marked their course. The wind was blowing in from the south and the temperature had dropped by three degrees.

There was no need for words. From the beginning, both of them had known that their night would end in the love hotel on Pampa Street. That is why it was odd when Zárate had given the driver a different address. We need to be careful, he'd said. Kezelman, feeling awkward, smiled.

They had to walk 300 metres. After a few steps Zárate nonchalantly placed his arm round her shoulder. She turned her head and kissed his hand. In that instant, in that very instant, despite the enormous effort she'd been making, she began to lose all her self-confidence. She doubted she was going to be able to go through with everything that lay ahead: hotel, bed, sex. It all seemed unnatural. The very thought of her skin brushing against his, even that was strange to her. She felt guilty and took a gulp of air before speaking. Her intention was to tell him no, that it wasn't going to happen this time, that she would understand perfectly if he thought her too neurotic and she was sorry but it was best to leave it there and go their separate ways. She was completely true to her thoughts; yet, just as she opened her mouth to utter the first word, Zárate spoke over her. He'd consulted the Chinese horoscope. From what he'd understood from it, they were predestined to be together.

They reached the hotel door. Marina Kezelman was shaking all over. She hadn't dared confess what she was feeling. While Zárate dealt with the paperwork (he passed his Visa card through a narrow slot in the dark glass), Kezelman, who was standing a few metres behind him, observed the movements: a calm but constant to and fro in a giant fish bowl. Once the logistics had been taken care of, Zárate waved her over. Come, he said. Second floor. They stepped into the lift and kissed deeply. Then he ran his tongue along the edge of Kezelman's jawbone and paused at her ear. She shuddered with pleasure. The tickling of his beard on her skin immediately triggered an image: a line of ants. She pushed the thought away with the fury of desire and grabbed Zárate by the hair. I hate you, she said. I hate you, she repeated. They stumbled into the room and tumbled onto the bed without removing the covers. They were delirious with excitement. For a second, once they got naked, they were breathless. It was midnight. Outside, the night was reaching its zenith.

Zárate roamed over Kezelman until he had nothing left. He was desperate. He felt the woman he was embracing could vanish into thin air. He bit her, squeezed her, yanked her hair. A ceiling mirror that reflected the scene back to them. Kezelman glanced at it from time to time. She was gauging the effectiveness of her caresses. She wrapped her legs around Zárate, trying to embed him in her body. After a while, they fell asleep. She dreamt precisely about what she was experiencing: the same characters, same scene, same smells. Then they showered together, using hardly any soap. They dressed in silence, rushing, somewhat self-consciously. They went through everything − unmade the bed − but failed to find her socks. First, they panicked, they thought it was the end of the world, but soon they were laughing. There was nothing on the face of the planet that could affect them.

They walked out to the street and each took a taxi home. Kezelman got into a gleaming Fiat Siena. She gave the driver her address and said the most direct route was via Libertador Avenue. Then she relaxed. Suddenly she felt deeply tired, as if she'd just run a marathon. She closed her eyes and rested the back of her neck against the seat. A strong smell of air freshener suffused the car. Kezelman felt that this synthetic fragrance, which at any other moment she would have found revolting, tugged her away from uncertainty. In other words, it was a gateway to everyday life. She reached for her handbag, took out a small mirror and looked at her lips. She moistened them with her tongue. She imagined that thousands of people – people crossing the city in taxis – were doing the same, exactly the same, at that very instant. To a point, she thought the harmony that brought them all together erased the very notion of individuality. Then, with her eyes still shut, she went a bit further still: she said to herself that she, with all her infidelity, neglect, secrets and guilt, was simply performing a cliché that humanity had repeated over and over again since the beginning of time.

Amer left the lawyer's office, walked a block under the pleasant mid-morning sun, and purchased a bottle of tonic water. He crossed the park and looked for a bench where he could sit and drink in peace. He was going through a stable period in his life in which happy events were falling neatly into place, one after another. He thought that the wisest thing to do was to enjoy the spell without overthinking it, and that this almost instinctive pleasure served not merely as an immediate boon, but precisely as a way of prolonging the sequence. He downed the tonic water and registered the liquid's icy trail down his throat. Since childhood, he had associated the bitter taste with the elimination of thirst. It was hardly an original idea but, in his case, unlike the commercials, it carried the force of truth.

He'd just received some excellent news from his lawyer. He had inherited money following the sale of a detached house, along with some land, in the locality of Carlos Casares. The succession process had been long, convoluted, and sometimes frustrating, but everything was finally under control. With that crisp money in reach, Amer suddenly hurtled into the future. Finishing his drink, he called Clara to share the news. In his excitement, he started making plans. He thought they could take a trip together and imagined somewhere by the sea under the sun. Let's go to Cuba for a week, he exclaimed. Clara rejected that idea outright, without hesitation. She'd reached a point in her teacher training when any change in her routine would hold her back. Feeling a bit baffled, Amer looked for any excuse to hang up. Three metres above his head, built into the branches of a white tipa tree, there was a huge nest, way too big for a single family of birds. Either it was an eagle's eyrie or some kind of shared nest.

He left the square along a gravel path, whistling the tango 'Tres amigos' which his mother used to sing when he was a boy. His pace was brisk, though he wasn't in a rush. In fact, he had taken the day off in order to think about the future. For the first time since he'd joined the group at Tobar García, he felt in his body – particularly in his legs, in the weight of his legs – the benefits of having quit smoking.

Without really knowing why, he went into a shoe shop and asked for a pair of loafers. He tried on three models, but none convinced him. Afterwards, following a certain scent – his sense of smell was as sharp as a dog's – he arrived at a chemist and bought a bottle of unisex cologne, the same one that the assistant was wearing. Back on the street, he unwrapped the package, opened the bottle and dabbed some on his neck and wrists. There was nothing that could stop him, nothing. He had the money behind him; that and a bullet-proof sense of self. At noon, he ate a tuna sandwich in a Subway. He made use of the break to make a dentist's appointment, and to phone Clara again. They agreed to meet that same evening. She had a training session somewhere in the north of the city. They both liked the idea: they would go to find out more about the apiculture classes at the University City campus and then go straight to celebrate.

Finding the bee place wasn't easy. Once they reached the university, they crossed the car park and walked along the side of Pavilion 3, finding themselves in scrubland. They crossed a wire fence, then a ditch filled with muddy water. Several lapwings flew by low, protecting their nest. In a clearing, they spotted the hives. Beyond them, among eucalyptus trees, was a tin shed with its doors wide open. They went up, searching for someone to show them around but, as they approached, a black dog emerged from the tall grass and dashed towards them. Instinct prevailed: Clara used Amer as her shield; Amer covered his face with his arms as if the animal were a bomb. The dog growled and barked but didn't attack them. Its ferocity was a show of what it was capable of. A few seconds later, a very tall guy with dishevelled red hair shot out of the shed. Neón, he shouted once. The dog froze, and from one moment to the next turned around and slunk back into the same bit of scrubland from where it had come.

They sat in the shade at a rustic wooden table and drank mate. The apiculture course would start the following week and it lasted three months. It covered everything: work regulations, protection, handling of hives, common pests and – time permitting – an introduction to the commercial world of honey. Amer listened carefully. Dusk was falling. Noises – crickets and especially the purring of an engine – imbued the scene with an unreal atmosphere. You have to be ready to handle 100,000 bees, said the red-haired man. He wore two metal hoops, one on his nose and the other one on his earlobe, although in his case, the ornaments didn't heighten his beauty. Quite the contrary: they were mistakes made bearable by habit.

If there was a reason why Karl found himself in front of the computer just then, browsing through an esoteric website, tossing three virtual coins up six times in the virtual air, it was because he'd heard his wife go on about the I Ching. It held his concentration for a good while. He was wearing his glasses. He'd tried to fix them with sticky tape, but they were still crooked: the left side sat below the right one. This detail made the German look ridiculous – he was a caricature of himself, like cross-eyed people – but above all it caused a refractive flaw in his eyesight. The world, once crystal clear, now seemed lacklustre, unfocused. And this new reality, unbeknownst to him, had a direct impact on his mood. He continued with the oracle and came to the hexagrams that pertained to his life: 42, birth, 17, continuity. He read them meticulously but couldn't make much sense of it all. From the whole thing just two words stayed with him: movement and sacrifice. He used these to shape his own version of the future.

He closed the computer, pushed the table towards the wall and took off his shoes. He lay on his back on the floor and closed his eyes, trying to concentrate on his breathing. The air whistled resonantly as it moved in and out of his nose. Once he'd managed to focus, he raised his legs, passed them over his head and tried to reach the floor with his feet. He'd learnt this position at the Indra Devi Foundation. Ever since his subway episode, his body had ached, particularly his joints and back. The pain was so strong that it sometimes woke him up in the night. He hadn't seen a doctor because he'd quickly observed the benefits of yoga. As soon as he settled into the first asana, relief came. Then, when he went to repeat the posture for the third time, his foot bumped into a lamp on top of a cabinet, knocking it over. It fell to the ground and the glass shade shattered into smithereens. With his concentration also broken, the practice was over.

He went to his son's bedroom. Simón was absorbed in a computer game. On screen, everything merged into a single image: exterminating beams and bright flashes. Do you want something to eat? Karl asked. The sun filtered in through the blind, tracing parallel lines on the wooden floor. Karl persisted: Shall I make us something? How about I fry some eggs? The air smelled of sweat, or of burnt wire and sweat. Simón jerked his head in answer, a movement that Karl could interpret either as a yes or a no. He went for the former. Simón was wearing only his underpants and the official football t-shirt for Racing Club. It was 12:40 p.m. Some neighbour was listening to a ballad by Iva Zanicchi.

The German boiled some rice and rested the wooden spoon against the edge of the pan. Three minutes before the rice was ready, he heated some oil in a frying pan and cracked the eggs into it. He adjusted the intensity of the flame and washed up the utensils as he finished with them. He'd placed a glass of water on top of the fridge and took an occasional sip. The counter was clear apart from a sliced lemon and a small jar of saffron.

Once he'd dished up the food, he lined up the plates, took a photo with his phone and sent it to Marina Kezelman. Seconds later he received a reply: a happy face emoji. Karl set the living room table and called his son. Lunch is ready, he shouted. But Simón didn't appear. Karl called again, to no avail. Then he went to get him. Simón was now wearing shorts and a bandana with the colours of the Jamaican flag. He'd been in the same position for a long while now: his buttocks poised on the edge of his chair, his full attention on the game. He looked younger than he was. Simón, food's on the table, Karl persisted. The boy struggled to lift his gaze from the screen. He stared at his father for a couple of seconds and said: I'm not hungry. Get me an apple. Karl blinked three times consecutively and left a sentence unfinished. He brought the plate to the room. I've made this! Simón was still lost in the web. I've made us lunch, Simón, I've made us lunch, Karl exclaimed. Infuriated by his son's indifference, he waved his arms, paced around him. Nothing worked. So he lost his patience. He grabbed Simón by the shoulders and shook him as if trying to wake him up. The boy – less out of rancour than out of astonishment – threw an open-handed blow at his father. The slap landed flat on the German's neck. Karl leapt backwards and unplugged the computer with a swift movement. You're for it, he said. Simón threw himself on the bed and burst into tears.

Back in the living room, Karl wolfed down his son's plate as well as his own. He devoured the scraps with a biscuit and downed two glasses of wine. While he ate – he chewed like a Neanderthal – he could hear Simón's muffled sobs, mouth pressed into the pillow. Sorrow floundered in his chest. In an attempt to distract himself, he opened Google on his phone. He learnt that the last soldiers to surrender in the Second World War were Japanese, a lieutenant and a private. Both in the same year, 1974, with an eight-month gap between them.

She was on a battlefield, far from any trench. Marina Kezelman took Simón to school. She was wearing a pleated skirt and an embroidered blouse. On the way, she told her son about her work. When rabbits run free in the countryside they eat mushrooms, which grow in damp conditions. I measure those conditions and talk about them with other people who do research on the subject, Kezelman explained. The boy rolled his eyes. He was fed up. Dad's cooking is awful, he said. Karl was a responsible father, Kezelman replied, and added that he, Simón, shouldn't be complaining about nonsense. But she stumbled, distracted, on a detail of her own rebuke. She paused to get back on track. Once she remembered where she'd left off, she went back to talking about rabbits.

Back home, she sat down at the computer. Before she could start on the first email, she saw her husband was leaving for a rehearsal. He seemed taller than usual. Usually people shrink over time, she thought, but this guy's getting bigger. It was a fact: everything around Karl tended to lose its sparkle, its elegance. Kezelman asked him when he'd be back and, stroking his face, sent him on his way. She watched him from the doorway as he waited for the lift: oboe hanging from his shoulder, oversized shirt, a face that made you think of Lou Ferrigno, that actor who used to play The Incredible Hulk. The second she was on her own, she texted Zárate. She made herself a cup of tea and placed it next to the keyboard. She spent some time moving the cursor and staring blankly at the screen. The morning breeze crept in through the window and took a couple of turns before merging with the smells of the house.

At noon, there was an abrupt change in the air. An intensification, a surge of vigour. Kezelman had read Zárate's amorous message ten times and had replied to a few emails, but only two stuck in her mind: one sent by her boss, asking for a document on Formosa that she'd already sent; the other, a promotional ad from some kind of esoteric school, which had just opened three blocks from their home.

A short while later, at 12:26 p.m., Marina Kezelman received another email. It was from Simón's school and it described the menu for the week. Today, she read, he'd have sausages and mashed potatoes and fruit jelly for pudding. When she was done reading, a car alarm went off in the street, a series of piercing noises that varied every ten seconds. She couldn't absorb them into the auditory background. Marina Kezelman bit her lip and tried to concentrate on an article about sunspots. But the noise got to her. She searched for cotton wool, kneaded two little balls and stuck them in her ears. Useless. Maybe, she thought, she could escape the aggravating sound if she tried doing something else instead. She transcribed her field notes into an Excel sheet. In a yellow column, the numbers from all the rows came together to a single sum: 3,227. Balance comes about when factors clash, Marina Kezelman thought. An image came to her: two squads of molecules fighting on unstable ground that slanted right or left, depending on the clamour of the battle.

She placed two corn cobs inside a plastic bag and put them in the microwave. Indifferent to cutlery, she ate them with her hands and wiped her mouth using the same tissues she'd used to blow her nose. She'd been allergic to most things since childhood, a condition that had gradually altered her features. In her appearance, a hypersensitivity to dust mites was as significant as genetics: Marina Kezelman was a version of her own mother, but with the facial features dilated – thickened and slightly reddened – particularly around her lips and nostrils. Except for the affected areas, her skin was fresh, healthy looking, as if she were ten years younger and she'd just emerged from a dip in a mountain stream.

Once she'd finished eating, she sat back down at the computer, but her attention wandered. She imagined that if she were to research something in depth, the rigour of the task would force her to concentrate. She browsed the Internet for a scientific article and began to read it. After ten minutes, her search led her to a video of an eighty-two-year-old German biologist. He was talking about a nature reserve in the Amazon. A conservationist, he grounded his ideology more in his experience than in his erudition. He described his trips to the Congo and the time he'd spent in the Brazilian rainforest. Marina Kezelman found this man's life more attractive than her own, which she considered paltry and predictable.

She decided to head outside. She bought herself an ice cream and ate it under the shade of a chinaberry tree. Then she walked briskly for three blocks and found herself turning into the esoteric school that had sent her the promotional email. A guy with a long scruffy beard greeted her at reception. He seemed harmless to her, the most harmless man she'd ever seen. He looked like a deer, but not just any deer; the kind of deer that lived in the depths of the Australian forests, the one she'd seen less than a week ago in a National Geographic documentary. As the guy described classes, schedules and costs, Marina Kezelman thought of Zárate. She thought about the sharpness of his features, the two creases that framed his mouth, his prominent jaw, and she thought about the moment they'd spent together. Last time, in the hotel, she'd given him everything that needed to be given, and that was precisely why, when they stepped out onto the street, she'd felt empty, utterly empty. She understood that there was nothing left in her anymore, and that this, far from being a surprise, was something she'd been seeking for a while now. She touched a finger to her lips. Suddenly she felt as if she were climbing up the curve of a spiral that was taking her all the way to a summit. That place, apparently so remote, was in fact her starting point. Standing on that vertex, she told herself, she'd start to make decisions.

He settled the glass eyes into the cavities. He used a tiny silicone brush to touch them up with vegetable oil. The smallest of details: two strokes to the right, two to the left. That was his secret: it gave a sparkle to the gaze. Now the otter looked different. A heavy whiff of borax hovered in the air. Breaking the resistance of both the glass and the net curtain, the solid afternoon light shone in through the window.

Amer took three steps back from the table and studied his work from a distance. He was satisfied. The scalpel mark at the end of the abdomen was hardly noticeable; no one would pay it any attention. The facial expression was more than well executed. The otter really seemed like a living creature; with the vividness of its own features added to the artist's skill, it gracefully avoided affectation. Indeed, the symphony of gestures appeared to have come to a halt just a few seconds earlier. Its attitude – the shape of the snout, the placing of the eyes – meant it had escaped the unnatural rictus, that formidable fixity of death. The otter – in the false tension of its reconstructed body – demanded different surroundings, it defined them, and that interplay with reality forged a vital spark. It was an embalmed animal, to be sure, but it asserted itself from a place of uncertainty. And this is what lay at the heart of Amer's success. He knew that much, and that's what had him smiling now.

The following day he and Clara drove the Galaxy to Carlos Casares. The plan was to visit the house and the small patch of land he'd inherited from an aunt, his father's oldest sister, a pale-skinned Hungarian who smoked like a chimney and always wore her grey hair in a bun. Amer had heard about this piece of land ever since he was a child – the vines, the big shed, the fifteen hectares of vegetable crops – but he'd never been. They drove up a dirt road that got narrower and narrower until it ended at a gate. A sceptical-looking lad wearing a beret, Facundo Maya, was waiting for them. His wariness dissolved as soon as they passed around the first mate.

Maya introduced them to the employees, seven in total, and showed them around the facilities. Then he took them to see the surrounding area in a white 4x4. He stopped metres from a watering hole, by the ruins of a building. This is all that's left of Fort Urbero, he said. Amer nodded, although he'd never heard the name before. A mass of clouds shifted slowly across the sky. Maya spoke with a peculiar tone of voice that made everything he said sound insignificant or false. He told them he used to run marathons and that he was a direct descendant of the founder of the town. He had a long neck, with a prominent Adam's apple, and his eyes sat very close together. Amer thought that a guy like him could either be a great help or complicate everything. We'll just have to see, he said to himself. In the distance, on the main road, trucks loaded with cattle drove past in both directions.

In the car on the way back, Clara was more sombre than usual, responding curtly to Amer's remarks. They stopped at a café in a service station for some coffee. She stared out of the window: the empty forecourt, beyond it the tyre repair shop. A cluster of weathered trees completed the scene. The skin under her eyes was yellow and haggard, lacking in definition, as if indifference had taken a greater toll there than on any other part of her body. Since she wasn't saying a word, Amer broke the silence and spoke for two. He said he'd like to set up beehives on the farm, that he was going to talk to the red-haired guy from the course to ask for some guidance that very week, that he was eager to get on with it. Amer had resolved to build a reality where Clara would fit; he was carrying a pipe dream on his shoulders. He let a week go by and headed back to the University City campus.

He arrived at 5:12 p.m. on a Tuesday and spoke to the red-haired guy. He asked him about the requirements for setting up an apiary. There was a coolness in the air and everything suggested that a storm would break out in a couple of hours, if not sooner. The red-haired guy seemed uncomfortable. As he talked, he washed a metal grill in a large sink. This time, his hair was tied up in a ponytail and he wore a working shirt with the sleeves cut off. The apiary needs to be set up 200 metres away from any housing, public thoroughfares and enclosed animals, he said. He made a movement with his head as if to imply that what he'd just said was obvious. In his opinion, he added, the best brands of hives were Langstroth and Jumbo. He mentioned the importance of water, moisture and polleniferous vegetation. Amer fixed his eyes on the beekeeper's fingernails. They were like claws. He imagined this detail was the symptom of a dormant illness that would manifest itself before long. There's a store in Moreno that has a good range and isn't too pricey, said the red-haired guy. The afternoon was waning. Amer tried to offer him something for the advice, but the beekeeper acted swiftly: he undid his ponytail, shook out his hair, and tied it back up again. All in less than a minute. That was his answer. Then he sighed, relieved.

It was during a rehearsal that he noticed his chin was trembling. Must be the reed, he thought. Yet when he checked it over – he examined it in the pause between two movements – he confirmed that it was in perfect condition. He reckoned that the problem had to be with the keys. It must be a reverberation from one of the levers, a sort of tremor that travelled up the body to the mouthpiece, and into his mouth. The vibration was physically uncomfortable; worse, it affected the sound, turning it nasal. They were playing Schumann's *Fantasie in C major*. Karl was trying in earnest to fix the problem but every time he began to play, he felt himself losing control of his jaw, and his bones began to shake of their own accord. Upon his second entrance, he noticed that two violinists glanced at him in surprise. Twelve bars later, they whispered something to each other. The first impression was that the instrument was out of tune. Listening carefully, however, and trying to isolate the oboe from the rest of the orchestra, it was clear that it was rather a quivering of the musical notes – which seemed to be emerging half-chewed – that weakened and decoloured them.

When the rehearsal ended, Ferlán, the conductor, beckoned to Karl. He leant against a column and asked him what the matter was. His tone was friendly, as if he were more worried about Karl than about how the piece was coming together. Do you realise how you sound, Karl? The proscenium smelt of disinfectant and damp cleaning rags. Ferlán was as tall as the German and blinked less than other humans. Karl replied with whatever leapt to mind:

he was going through a personal crisis and it was having an impact on his playing. What's up? Ferlán asked. Karl shrugged his shoulders. His excuse had run dry in a single phrase and now the director was demanding the details. Someone on the stage was playing the piano, repeating chords over and over again, and as the music reached them, it influenced their conversation in some obscure way. Unconsciously, they were both performing roles in a scene that wasn't entirely real. Against this setting, the German said he'd felt for some time that things weren't right with his wife, that something between them had broken and that he didn't think it could be repaired. The maintenance staff switched off an overhead light, and Ferlán and Karl suddenly felt uncomfortable talking in the gloom. Karl leaned his head against the wall – a faint light entered from the corridor to the dressing rooms – and Ferlán felt awkward at their unsought intimacy.

Once back in the street, Karl recorded an audio message for Marina Kezelman. He told her about his shakiness during rehearsal. And he told her he loved her. Somehow, uttering these words was a way to mend the lies he'd just made up.

It was a bright day, neither hot nor cold, so he decided not to take the subway. He walked until he reached Sarmiento and halted at the window of a shop that sold musical instruments. He hesitated for three seconds and walked in. He purchased a hand-painted set of Andean pan-pipes for his son. Then he hopped on the bus home. As soon as he got off, he thought of making some fresh juice. He walked into a greengrocer and was served by a slightly hunched guy who reminded him of himself fifteen years earlier. He asked for two kilos of oranges and a grapefruit. For the first time, he felt that as he moved away from music – which lately had meant the orchestra – he plunged into life more fully, as if he were diving into a strong, alluring sea. There was nothing like the warmth of the afternoon sun on your face: a freedom tarnished by the memory of what had happened earlier in the day.

He squeezed the grapefruit and one orange. He had to bend down slightly: the kitchen worktop was too low for him. Karl's size quarrelled with most spaces. He was convinced that modern architects designed buildings with poor proportions. This explanation cast a kind of spell against his height. He poured the juice into a tall glass and went to the living room to drink it. He placed his feet on the coffee table and stayed there, savouring. The house was empty and airy. He felt a gentle breeze from the right. The window had been left slightly ajar and the curtain fluttered every three seconds, coaxing calm thoughts. According to the rippling cloth, the universe was an amenable place. Karl, softened by the mood of those curtains, lowered his head, almost without realising it, until his gaze was fixed on the remaining juice in the glass. His thoughts drifted into a delta of striations, a foamy draughts board. It was a primitive landscape: uneven pathways among dykes formed by bits of pulp.

He had left the peel on the kitchen worktop. When Karl went to the fridge for some ice, he saw the ants had made an advance. It wasn't the first time he'd seen them, but now their spitefulness repulsed him. There were hundreds, moving at great speed. They seemed to be sprouting from everywhere. Karl wiped the granite surface with detergent, followed by insecticide. When he opened the lid of the bin to get rid of the waste, he saw a paper bag from the chemist with something inside, something long with a rounded tip. He was puzzled by how neatly wrapped it was; it had even been sealed with parcel tape. He hesitated for an instant, then shook it gently. Gaining confidence, he picked it up with his fingertips and observed it closely. Then he set it down on the worktop and opened it. What he saw made his heart beat faster. It was the orange vibrator he'd given Marina Kezelman for her birthday. He was stunned. For a while, he stood there overwhelmed until, in a surge of energy, he wrapped the dildo back up just as he'd found it and put it away in the drawer of his bedside table. Then he lay down on the sofa to read a biography of Mahler. He tried and failed to focus. He kept having to double back, re-reading each page three times. After twenty minutes of this, he placed the book on the table and left the house to buy beer.

Following a meeting at the Ministry, Marina Kezelman and Zárate went out for lunch at a restaurant downtown. They sat in a booth and ordered red wine and sparkling water. From the outset, their moods introduced a stiffness to the encounter. It was the first time their interaction didn't flow naturally. A plate of sliced cheese was brought to the table as an appetiser. Marina Kezelman started rolling up the slices and eating them one by one. Meanwhile, Zárate talked about his daughter. A week earlier he'd bought her a fish tank with three fish; only one had survived. Zárate thought that an excess of chlorine had killed the other two. They shared a German dish, sausages with potatoes. It was too much for them. They couldn't finish it. Outside, the sky was free of clouds and the sun was gradually softening the asphalt. In the restaurant, however, it was night-time. Neither the brightness nor the bustle of the day filtered in. The lights were on and everyone moved comfortably in the unexpected interval of calm.

My life is falling apart, said Kezelman. Zárate sought distance. He leaned back in the seat and wiped his mouth with his napkin. He wriggled his eyebrows by way of an answer. I want to leave Karl, she went on. At that very moment, a waiter walked by with a plate, trailing the scent of shellfish. We must take things slowly, replied Zárate, and pressed a finger between his eyes as if he had sinusitis. Kezelman took a sip of water. She paid attention to the background music: Rita Lee was singing a bossa nova cover of a Beatles song. She felt, more than ever before, that the world was a vulgar place. I think about you all day long, she said.

They ordered coffee and accepted the glass of champagne offered by the waiter. Kezelman explained that she could no longer sleep in the same bed as her husband. She'd thought of hinting at what was going on. Just a hint, not the whole picture. We have to be mindful of others, said Zárate and inhaled deeply through his nose. Karl is the least of my worries. He's strong, he's a survivor, said Kezelman. She didn't say: I think Karl's an idiot. Nor did she say: neither Karl nor you are worth it.

They stepped out into the street and walked for two blocks. Zárate headed into a car park and Marina Kezelman continued walking. The farewell kiss was barely a brush on the lips. Kezelman made a mental list of her obligations for the rest of the day and suddenly felt crestfallen. Her chiropractic appointment was in an hour's time. She focused on the immediate future in order to stay in control. Her rhythm was different to the city's, marginally slower, and that small, almost indistinguishable discordance meant that reality, as she saw it, was out of sync. Everything looked the same, yet ever so slightly altered, as if out of focus. Soon enough, a sense of unsteadiness came over her, and Marina Kezelman didn't want to face it on the street.

She went into a café, ordered an espresso and rushed into the toilet to wash her face. She removed the two rings she was wearing and placed them to one side of the sink. At that very instant, she remembered a Japanese hairdresser who used to come to her house when she was a girl. She'd cut both her mother's hair and her own. As she worked – she would grab a lock between her fingers, apply the scissors and release it again with a certain disdain – she'd tell stories, all of which she'd conclude with a saying. There was one she used to repeat: passion always beats fear. This phrase now echoed in Marina Kezelman's mind. The resolution of this maxim was directly related to what she was going through, she had no doubt about that. She clenched her teeth and swung open the toilet door. She entered the main café area, which felt like a huge boxing ring, with spotlights glaring on the crowd of adversaries. Yes, they were all enemies, or rather, any of them could become one. Marina Kezelman blinked three times, as if she'd got something in her eye, and walked to her table.

Her coffee had been served. She took a sip and swiftly pulled her phone out of her bag. She handled it with her fingertips, almost with her fingernails. Something in her dexterity – Kezelman was a spider, subtle and exacting – had to do with technological progress: quick fingers and virtual keyboard were one and the same. She opened the I Ching app and asked a question. Lately, all her conundrums took the same form. The answer came: Perchance the army carries corpses in the wagon; determination and order shall prevail over mishaps. She was determined. She sent a message to Karl – I want to talk to you – and asked him to meet her somewhere near their house. She was certain that the neutrality of café bars would encourage fruitful dialogue.

Amer woke up before his alarm went off: urine on the floor tiles, dampness on his face, toothpaste on his teeth. He went to the kitchen and heated up coffee from the day before. He poured it into a mug and added some milk. He sat on a stool at a folding table. He took a sip and smoothed the neck of his t-shirt. The air coming through the window was mingling with the smell of borax. He sent a WhatsApp audio to Clara. He told her he was going to buy the hives as well as a number of other items for the apiary. Her answer came right away. She said she wanted to go with him, that she felt like going out for a bit and spending time together. They agreed to meet at 3 p.m. in a café a few steps from the station.

Between messages, Amer spread strawberry jam on his toast. He chewed calmly as he listened to Clara's messages, focusing on her voice. She was recounting things a little haphazardly. She told him about a dream she'd had. She was with her family and suddenly she began suffering an attack – a kind of a stroke – that paralysed the left side of her body. Her mouth was aslant and she was unable to move one arm and one leg. In the dream, someone took her to the hospital, where she was placed on a metal chair and left alone in a doctor's surgery with high ceilings. She insisted that someone call Amer but no one could understand what she was saying. It was horribly distressing, she concluded. Amer savoured his coffee. He liked the thought that Clara needed him in her dreams.

He stayed busy that day, tackling one task after another. He placed the otter on a wooden stand, gluing it in place with contact adhesive and then securing it with two nails in each leg. He stared at it and made a few small adjustments. He paid special attention to the snout area. He wanted to bring out the join at the edge of the lips so as to accentuate its expression. So deep was his focus that he lost track of time. By 2 p.m. he was starving. He ate a green apple and a banana. Then he poured milk into a glass and tried to drink it so quickly that he spilt it all over himself. Fucking hell, he shouted in fury. He wiped the kitchen floor with a cloth and went to change his t-shirt. He stepped into the bathroom to clean the rest of milk that had gone down his chin. He looked at himself in the mirror. His torso was naked and his hair dishevelled. The bags under his eyes were darker than usual.

Shit, I'm going to be late, he exclaimed out loud, and rushed out the door, heading for the café where he'd agreed to meet Clara. He walked for half a block before realising he didn't have the address with him. He ran back, grabbed the note from the fridge where it was stuck with a magnet, and went downstairs again. He hailed a taxi and asked the driver to head down Constituyentes Avenue. When he was two blocks away, he got a message from Clara, two in fact. The first one lasted just three seconds, and he heard her breathing hard: she was trying to catch her breath so she could speak. In the second one, she said she wouldn't be able to make it because her sister's dog, a Belgian shepherd, had attacked a neighbour's poodle. As soon as he'd finished listening to the messages, Amer called Clara, but she didn't pick up. He sent an audio message. Keep me posted, he said. Clara sent a thumbs-up emoji.

Amer sat at the bar and ordered a coffee. He felt a strong urge to smoke, stronger than he'd ever felt since he quit. In fact, before getting on the train, he bought himself a pack of Marlboro which he ended up throwing away, unopened. He endured the journey like a prison sentence: he was supposed to take this train with her. On top of it all, he struggled to find the beekeeping supplies shop. When he finally got there, he didn't buy a thing: he just consulted prices and accepted the card of an assistant who seemed reliable.

Marina Kezelman chose a Starbucks to talk to Karl. The conversation was brief. Offering only half-truths, she deftly dodged reproaches and prevailed in her will as if it were an abstract thing rather than a personal choice. As if disintegration were a law of matter and spirit alike. They agreed that he would leave the house that very same day and they'd work out everything else the following week. When she had nothing left to say, Kezelman stroked Karl's cheek. Her gesture suggested that she was very sorry, but such implacable decisions had to be accepted quickly. The German stood up, resolute, like nothing had happened. He walked the three blocks back to their house. He packed his clothes in a suitcase, the scores in a bag and the music stand inside the oboe case. He placed everything next to the door. Then he went to the fridge, poured himself a large glass of grapefruit juice and downed it in one long swig. His movements were automatic, one after the other, and this – the contiguity of each action rather than his own effort to move – was what ensured he kept going. As he paced back and forth, he thought about how best to resolve his short-term dilemma. He called a colleague from the orchestra, a cello player, explained the situation and asked if he could stay with him for a couple of days.

The last thing he did in his house was to look for a tranquiliser so he'd be able to sleep that night. He rooted around in the medicine cabinet and some other drawers in the bathroom. Having no success, he took three tablets of a muscle relaxant containing Pridinol instead. He soon felt dizzy but lucid. Before leaving – the door was open, his hand on the latch – he stood there for a moment, motionless. Then he turned on his heels, returned to the bedroom and retrieved the vibrator wrapped in the chemist's bag. Next he went into the bathroom to collect his toothbrush, but in his haste he took Marina Kezelman's as well. He put everything in the outer pocket of his suitcase. He left the door unlocked behind him. Outside, the street lamps had come on. He raised his head and saw halos round the bulbs.

He spent only three days at the cello player's house. He didn't want to impose. The guy was generous but he lived in a one-bedroom flat and used the space where Karl slept to teach private lessons. From there, he moved to temporary accommodation on Oro Street, above a mini-market. He didn't last long there either. Soon after, he changed neighbourhoods. He managed to find a flat on the tenth floor across from Plaza Sinclair and there he stayed.

The separation hit Karl square in the face and loosened his teeth. He had to maintain a gum treatment routine that took up more than half an hour of his day. What's more, his loneliness reinforced his status as a foreigner. In fact, he got lost twice in Buenos Aires, the second time just three streets away from his house. During the first few months of his new life, he thought about returning to Germany, but knew that he couldn't live so far away from his son. He discovered Xanax and redrew his ontological map around the pills. He got used to living in a muffled reality, without nuances or extremes. He moved around like a sleepwalker. The good thing was that his jaw stopped shaking and the sound of his playing improved. One day, Ferlán congratulated him for his new-found concentration. The German had grown out his beard (though it was rather patchy), had lost five kilos and his eyelids seemed to be covered by a layer of varnish, an effect of the tranquilisers.

One warm Saturday, he went to pick up Simón. They spent all morning walking round the parks in Palermo. Then Simón said he wanted to go to McDonald's. Karl tried in vain to dissuade him. After lunch, they went back to the park. They sat down near a lake to sunbathe until, all of a sudden, the situation started to crumple. The conversation became riddled with awkward silences. Within a few minutes, Simón's face had changed: he looked bored. I want to go home, he said. Karl explained that he'd arranged with his mother for Simón to spend the night at his place. The boy shook his head. There was something defiant in his reaction. I don't want to, he said. When he dropped him off at Kezelman's house, Karl told her what had happened, how Simón had rejected him. It's not rejection, she replied. You have to start paying attention to what other people want.

When the cat's away, the mice will play, he'd been told. Amer was a methodical man: he'd set a date and make all the arrangements for the trip, but when the time came to leave, he'd produce any old excuse to stay in the city. To compensate, he'd talk to Facundo Maya every other day. He'd call around noon, listen to what he had to say – Maya's updates were always disjointed but detailed – and make some minor decision or other. When it came to important matters, he'd unfailingly follow the overseer's advice. I agree, he'd say, let's go for it. During their calls, Amer could make out the sounds of the countryside in the background: the song of a great kiskadee, a dog barking, machines clattering along in the fields. He'd use these elements to construct the scene, the place his words were reaching. They were also his way of laying claim to the farm, of making a commitment that was all the stronger for its imaginary nature. The last time he'd spoken to the overseer, Amer had informed him that he'd be setting up the beehives within a month at most. It was the right moment; he was certain of that. Maya was so enthusiastic about the project that Amer felt suspicious. He worried that there was something nasty hiding behind such frank good will. We have to place the hives 200 metres from the waterhole, that's the best place for them, said the overseer. That's exactly what I was thinking, lied Amer. Maya guffawed. Indeed, he was so candid that it cleared up Amer's doubts about this guy he hardly knew. He had the urge to invite him to go to the apiculture place together. But something – an affected sense of caution – stopped him. He remained silent for three seconds – did it really make sense to bring the overseer to the city? – and during that instant, brief as a sigh, he heard the mooing of a cow from the other end of the line. What's that? he asked. A cow? Maya pretended not to understand. A cow? he repeated. We have cows now? Maya tried to explain. He said something about a vet friend and some pasture land. Nothing seemed credible, yet Amer didn't insist. I have to go and find out what's going on there in person, he thought. I smell a rat.

The following day he got up at 6:45 a.m. He browsed through his emails as he sipped on some coffee. A meeting at the museum had been cancelled, so his afternoon was free. He poked his head out of the window and felt a deep sense of wellbeing. A few clouds dotted the sky. His elation was so intense that when he lowered his gaze to the street and saw it so close by, the sense of bliss was transformed, as if by magic, into anxiety. He leaned against the wall and texted Clara: I'm off to buy the hives. Do you want to come with me? She refused immediately. She had plans with her sister, an activity in at a school for deaf-mute kids. There was something methodological about her evasiveness. Amer stuck his chest out and moved about like a superior man. Fuck her, he thought. I'll go on my own.

He killed some time in the same café as the last time. Every now and then, he looked towards the door as if she were about to walk in. Then he got on the train and quickly grabbed a window seat. He half-closed his eyes. Opening them fully again – the train hadn't yet moved – he saw a pile of bricks, a bucket and a car battery all lying on the platform. At that moment, the doors shut and the formation lurched into movement. The mechanical trudge, that flurry of activity, led him to imagine a horse – a brown, spirited, almost martial horse – that metamorphosed into a cow. What dodgy business had that idiot

Maya got mixed up in? he wondered. It hadn't been long since Amer had inherited this land and he was already fed up with grabbing the bull by the horns.

Kezelman left the I Ching for the Tarot. It seemed more accessible to her. She found an app that made her write a question and choose a card; ten seconds later, it would provide an answer. Generally speaking, her questions involved Zárate. Their relationship was treading water: he was still married and, as far as Kezelman could see, obsessed with his daughter's health. The dog attack had left the girl with problems in her right hand, namely numbness and tingling. Zárate was like a broken record: he wouldn't talk about anything but his daughter's woes. One day, someone recommended he try a doctor from Boston who was a hand specialist, one of the best in the world. Zárate didn't think twice. He organised the trip in no time. Kezelman didn't want to engage; she'd shrug her shoulders whenever he asked for her opinion on any of it. In private, however, she felt that going to the US to see this doctor was over the top. The dramatisations of a guilty father, she thought. She always sensed her lover was timorous and opportunistic, but an episode at work had recently justified this view. Kezelman had intercepted an email in which Zárate badmouthed a colleague in the hope of earning the trust of the project manager. The discovery didn't push her away; it actually strengthened her desire for him. Zárate was like shifting sands. He thrived on uncertainty, and his ambiguity made him irresistible. He was the impossible man, which meant he was the one she wanted.

Marina Kezelman thought of herself as a bright woman, although she knew emotional strength was her strong suit. Nevertheless, when Zárate's family left for the US, she felt a desolation that she'd never experienced before. In an effort at self-preservation, she promised herself she wouldn't try to find anything out about the trip. In the end, though, her angst was stronger than her will. She went online and checked the flight details. The plane was leaving at 4:15 p.m. When the hour arrived, Marina Kezelman transformed into a different person. She went about her usual business, fulfilled her obligations, but her gaze had strayed into the distance, as if she were trying to recover a childhood memory. In actual fact, she was riveted by a picture created by her own imagination: Zárate walking through the airport hand in hand with his wife, their daughter three metres behind carrying a Kanken backpack. A simple scene that repeated itself in a fateful loop. To escape the torment, Marina Kezelman decided to get out of the house, do anything at all, be with other people. She went to pick Simón up from school and told him that they'd go out for lunch. Her son was taken aback: if there was one habit they respected it was going home after school to eat. They took a taxi up to the junction of Thames and El Salvador and went into a fast food place. They both ordered the same: a burger with bacon and cheddar cheese. Marina asked Simón how his day had been. The boy rolled his eyes in annoyance, but once he began to talk he got carried away with his own narration. He weaved together simple anecdotes that his nasal voice embellished in a way that made them sound extraordinary. Marina listened raptly. When the waiter left the soft drinks on the table, she entered a state that almost resembled calm. They ate without distractions. When the bill came, the waiter gave Simón a little plastic toy, a kind of Playmobil figure that the boy clutched tightly as if it had always been his. Unbeknownst to them, they had entered a raffle with their order number and had won third prize. Things are starting to fall into place, thought Kezelman.

It was an exceptional day for both of them. They got back home and sprawled out in bed to watch a Japanese anime film with a plot so bizarre that it put Marina to sleep in less than ten minutes. When she woke up, the sun was casting a rectangle of light across her face. She'd only been asleep for a short while, just four minutes, and uncomfortably – she'd been lying on her right arm. Reality had changed in the interim, now offering novelty and contrast. For one thing, Simón had got rid of the plastic figurine and was hugging his usual teddy bear. For another, the TV screen was no longer showing the anime images but rather the view from a cabin at the highest point of a fairground wheel. Marina Kezelman scrutinised the image like someone completing a task. The camera, fixed on top of a tripod, showed the panoramic views. A voiceover explained that the wheel, found on Linq Promenade in Las Vegas, was the tallest of its kind in the world. I want to go on one of those, said Simón. Marina Kezelman turned her head and looked at her son. She began to speak but gave up half-way through, as if her nap, that paltry respite, had sapped her of the ability to express ideas.

Marks of transience. On the living room wall there was a picture of Mozart and another of Schoenberg. They'd been cut out from a magazine and taped to the wall. Burnished by the afternoon sun, they had a yellowish tint and warped corners. Seated at a pine table eating jelly, Karl stared at each picture in turn, as if they concealed a specific meaning. The German felt good. He'd spent two hours studying a piece by Lebrun that he was going to play with a chamber group. Outside, the afternoon was an indefinable colour and the sky was clear, but something – a certain electricity in the air – complicated the transparency of the day. At 3 p.m., Karl savoured the last mouthful of jelly and sat still for a moment – not more than seven seconds – numbed by the clamour of the passing traffic. Then he leapt to his feet, grabbed his coat and went out. He'd agreed with his ex-wife that he'd go and fetch Simón by 4 p.m. Although he had plenty of time, he moved as fast as he could. He managed to jump on a bus just as it was leaving the stop and even got a seat. Next to him sat a local barber who'd recently cut his hair. Karl didn't recognise him straight away; when he did, though, he reintroduced himself. The barber seemed sullen at first, but wouldn't stop talking once he'd warmed up. He told Karl he was in the Argentinian Navy when the Falklands conflict broke out, and that he'd been sent to the islands to fight. Just as he'd embarked on recounting some horrendous episode that took place in Port Stanley, Karl got up. This is my stop, he said. The barber was stunned. He started to say something but changed his mind. The German got off and in three strides was far away.

Marina Kezelman had told her ex-husband about Simón's newfound fascination with Ferris wheels. We were watching a TV documentary that shows the wheel they have in Las Vegas and he got it into his head that he wants to ride on one, she explained. Karl, almost by chance, found out that there was one in a park just to the south of the city, in Moreno. He immediately decided to take his son there. He'll have fun, he thought.

He was standing at the door of his former house. Kezelman furrowed her eyebrows uneasily – a habit of hers – and handed Simón over like a parcel. She adjusted her son's coat – the lapels weren't quite straight – and told him to look after himself. Simón was well wrapped-up. He was wearing a blue rucksack with the Disney logo on it. They took a taxi up to Once, bought a bag of sweets and sat on a bench to wait for the train. The daylight had begun to falter. Simón told his dad about school. A few days before, a classmate, a kid called Zuno, had run into a glass sliding door. He'd gone straight through it. It was a miracle he didn't slash his throat, though his face was pitted with star-shaped marks. Karl paid attention to his son's story and to the movement on the platform. They boarded the train in a flock of other passengers. They weren't too nimble once they'd got on – they weren't sure which direction to walk in – but they managed to find seats, although not together. Fate had its consequences.

The trip felt long to both of them. For Simón, however, it was endless. Karl had jotted down the names of the sixteen stations they'd pass through before reaching their destination – one after the other in a column – and had given it to his son as a reference. But Simón was fickle: by the time they reached the fourth stop, he'd given up the count. The sensuality of the suburbs and the train's muted clattering made him sleepy. He played with his phone, bit his nails, looked out of the window sidelong:

the landscape was all grime and poverty.

They got off in Moreno and advanced as if walking a tightrope. They were dizzy from the train, unsteady on their feet. Karl amplified his enthusiasm – he talked about the park as if it were something lavish – and it made Simón cringe. The boy found everything about his father grotesque and exaggerated. Simón's nose was red from so much rubbing; it was his way of expressing disgust. Eight blocks from the station they found the entrance to the park: a metal gate more than ten metres high with a sign that read 'Trilenium Park'. They passed through it with determination, a bit anxious but striding firmly. They were gladiators. A heavy smell of fried food floated in the air, thick as a sheet of acetate. They bought ice cream and bolted it down. People milled around in groups, speaking loudly and laughing at anything. There was something offensive about their jollity. It pushed Simón deeper into himself. He grabbed hold of his father's hand and agreed to anything that Karl suggested. First, they went on the teacups ride – Simón couldn't imagine anything more hideous in the entire world – and then they tried some kart racing on karts that were impossible to steer. And finally they went up on the Ferris wheel. They sat on folding seats, one next to the other. As soon as they were locked in position – a security bar came down over their laps – Simón felt, for the very first time, something like camaraderie with his father. He was certain, although he struggled to understand it, that this experience, which still lacked any sort of specific expression, would somehow provide a refuge for him well into adulthood.

The mechanism started up with a creaking sound. My sweet boy, said Karl. And his words made it possible for them to relish what followed. Simón's mouth spread into a broad smile. For a moment, his face formed a perfect circle. He felt impatient and happy in a way that let him trust the suddenness of his excitement. The wheel moved slowly, very slowly, but they found themselves at the top within three minutes. Their chair rocked a little, and then came the sound they'd heard at the start: a deep clack, like ball bearings rolling together. Simón stretched his hand out towards the void, groping, feeling his way like a blind person, and one by one moved his fingers in the air. First the little finger: he pulled it into the centre of his hand, creasing his palm. Then the ring finger and the middle one. With the index finger, he paused. Suddenly, he lowered his hand to the bar and grabbed it with all his might, as if wanting to test the firmness of the world. Forgetting it all, he abruptly turned his head up and stared at the sky, a uniform expanse fixed at an hour: 6 p.m. There were a few clouds, maybe five, and one of them, stretching across the horizon, reminded him of his teddy bear's head. Solid and voluminous, it was arranged in a perfect curve. In that play of distances, the boy could make out a detail: a string of tiny clouds trailing into the distance. This image, both distinctive and fleeting, awakened something indefinable in his body; something, without knowing quite how, that brought him face-to-face with uncertainty. Perhaps this was why he quickly looked away, searching for a reference point. His gaze lit upon the sight of a passing train, its progress neither fast nor slow. The railway tracks were so close that he could make out the faces of the passengers through the windows: transient figures that entered his emotional mesh and anchored him to reality.

A lad was trying to sell bars of nougat as Amer fretted over rental prices. Despite the favourable change in his finances, he remained thrifty. He was reading a leaflet published by a state agency that detailed prices, square metres and amenities. His current place was falling to bits: the plaster on the walls was swelling up and bursting, the taps leaked and the wooden floor had begun to rot. His clothes smelled of damp. Adding insult to injury, a couple with two screaming children had moved into the flat next door a week earlier. Like a prisoner, he was counting the days.

By the time they got to Liniers, he was tired of looking at photos of flats. He convinced himself he didn't have the energy to move house. Partly to kill time but also to quell his anxiety, he called his landlord to let him know that a few things needed fixing. He then proceeded to list the following: some pipes had to be replaced, the roof terrace had to be sealed properly and the plaster on the walls needed attention. Oddly enough, the guy took in the tenant's complaints without saying a word. If it was fine by him, the landlord said, they would start work on the flat the following month. He had to go and find out a few prices, but nowadays with the Internet everything was easier and you could find some amazing offers if you were lucky. Amer hadn't expected such a ready response. Far from putting his mind at peace, such attentiveness sent him into a state of torpor, a kind of void from which he found it hard to emerge, as if he'd fallen inside an echo chamber. He rested his head against the window and closed his eyes. He didn't quite fall asleep, but his mind filled with a series of images threaded together by dream-logic: Clara was dancing flamenco with a group of Gypsies until she collapsed with exhaustion; one of the men – huge, with chains around his neck – helped her up and disappeared with her into a dark room. In this dream-like sequence, Amer was certain they were having sex but he couldn't get near enough to confirm. Something – his own immateriality – stopped him. He opened his eyes, disconsolate, and found it hard to focus. He saw some blurry images which sharpened after a few seconds: a row of seats with people in them, mostly half asleep. He observed his nails as he thought about sending a WhatsApp to Clara, but his phone started ringing as soon as he pulled it out of his pocket. It was Maya. He reckoned it would be bad luck to answer him after such an unpleasant dream. But he immediately rejected his own reasoning. Travel, as he well knew, can spark ridiculous ideas.

I'm on the train on my way to buy the things, Maya, what's up? asked Amer. The overseer, incapable of niceties, went straight to the point. The coop, it's a disaster, he said. From one day to the next, all of the hens had died. The disease had hit that same morning with the Sussex hens and soon moved on to the Leghorn. They blew up, literally. I burnt them all, just to be sure. There's not a single animal left. I reckon it's smallpox, said Maya, not much else it could be. Amer listened to what his employee had to say and opened his mouth. He sensed that beneath the story of the hens was another issue, the one that really mattered, but he could barely make it out. Shit, what a mess, he exclaimed. Please make sure you find out what happened, he commanded.

By the time the train left Paso del Rey, Amer had forgotten about everything, his attention completely absorbed by the view through the window. An extreme drought afflicted the landscape. All of a sudden, the train was crossing Namibia. Timber, tin roofs, wires, all cracked and faded. They formed a tarnished mass, a stage set that tried to disguise the desert. Amer shook his head as if trying to rid himself of the bitter taste the scene had left in his mouth. He rubbed his nose and looked up at the sky. There was nothing worthwhile on this planet. A cluster of clouds was drifting across the horizon to the west. Despite it all, Amer experienced a powerful sense of calm. After many years, things had fallen into place for him, and those clouds in that corner of the sky, so limpid and serene, were symbols of his state of mind. He looked at them again – not to decipher anything, but just to confirm that these good things had come to stay. He noticed that one of the clouds – abundant, intricate – was neatly curved, forming a shape much like the head of the grizzly bear he'd recently seen in the documentary. It sketched it precisely: an ovaloid form with two faintly ear-like edges. He sighed with pride. Somehow, that mass of vapour floating in the sky was his own work. At the end of the day, he was a taxidermist. When he lowered his gaze, he saw a funfair. A funfair! He was surprised. He stared at the Ferris wheel, struck by its design and stylishness – he mistook slowness for sophistication – as it turned in the air. He was so close to the ride that he could make out the faces of the people on it. He took his time to observe a woman with a large mouth, then a teenager wearing a fuchsia t-shirt, then a young couple. Yet what was remarkable, truly remarkable, is that he didn't see Simón, who at that very moment was turning his head – like a tiny satellite – slightly to the left. They missed each other by seven seconds. A mere seven seconds. A trifle, a smidgen, an iota, a fragment of time that, amid the vertigo of an evening that seemed to last forever, was absorbed like any other detail into the imperfections of the day.

CHARCO PRESS

Director & Editor: Carolina Orloff
Director: Samuel McDowell

charcopress.com

Fate was published on
90gsm Munken Premium Cream paper.

The text was designed using
Bembo 11.5 and ITC Galliard.

Printed in January 2020 by TJ International
Padstow, Cornwall, PL28 8RW using responsibly sourced paper
and environmentally-friendly adhesive.

MIX
Paper from
responsible sources
FSC® C013056